LEATHERMEN

LEATHERMEN

GAY EROTIC STORIES

EDITED BY
SIMON SHEPPARD

Published in the United States by Cleis Press, Inc.,
P.O. Box 14697, San Francisco, California 94114.

Printed in the United States.
Cover design: Scott Idleman
Cover photograph: Jackson Photografix
Text design: Frank Wiedemann
Cleis logo art: Juana Alicia
First Edition.
10 9 8 7 6 5 4 3 2 1

For William, again
And with thanks to Richard Labonté

Contents

EXPOSED

Aaron Travis

Craig stands naked before the mirror. What he sees frightens and excites him.

Earlier tonight, standing in the bathroom, clutching the electric clippers in his hand, he made up his mind to go through with it. He flipped the switch, then began to run the clippers slowly, methodically over the hard curving contours of his torso. The buzz vibrated through the heavy muscles of his chest, sending a tingle into his nipples; throbbed against the firm bands of muscle beneath his navel; nuzzled his armpits. Tufts of wispy brown hair fell to the floor.

The clippers were the first stage. They left behind a dusting of soft brown stubble, a foretaste of the smoothness to come, easy to brush away with the razor.

Shaving his chest is no big deal. Craig does it every so often—"Just to see how I'm coming along," he tells the guys at the gym. Craig lifts weights. Shaving reveals the contours of his pectorals and the ridges of his stomach, shows the mass and definition he's gained.

It also gives him an erotic thrill. After shaving his chest, he often stands for a long time before his bedroom mirror, oiling the denuded flesh, fascinated by the way the smooth, naked musculature gleams in the light. Shaving makes his nipples stand out. Large nipples, usually obscured by soft swirls of hair, are exposed and naked after the razor has made its pass.

Tonight is different. Tonight he decided to go all the way.

It's a fantasy that's been building in his head for months. To see himself completely hairless below the neck. He's thought of doing it many times, and always changed his mind at the last minute, just as the buzzing clippers are poised at the top of his pubic pelt. How could he show himself in the showers at the gym? Or alone with another man in his bedroom...?

It excites him, of course—the idea of another man seeing him that way. But it also embarrasses him. Laying it on the line. Revealing himself for what he is, in his fantasies at least: a nude muscleboy without a trace of hair on his body, as silky and smooth as a woman. The idea brings out a deep subservient streak in him. He imagines himself on his knees, naked, or better yet wrapped in leather straps that emphasize the width of his chest, the sleek overhanging fullness of his pectorals, the hardness of his cock standing up stiff from a smooth denuded crotch....

The vibration of the clippers running up his broad thighs, drawing closer and closer to his genitals, sent a wave of excitement through his cock. The shaft stood out, half-hard and throbbing, the whole time he ran the clippers through his pubic tuft and under his balls, watching in fascination and dread as the wiry hair fell away in clumps. He had done it. No turning back.

He shaved in the shower, lathering his body, scraping away wide swaths of hair, rinsing himself smooth and repeating the process until his testing fingertips could glide from his ankles to his underarms, slick as a wet bar of soap, without detecting a trace of stubble.

Afterward, the towel felt scratchy and strange against his flesh. He avoided looking at himself in the harsh glare of the bathroom mirror, waiting until he was ready.

In the bedroom, he lit the candles, then oiled his body from his shoulders to his feet. His hands slid up his calves and thighs with a new, incredibly sensual touch. Skin hard and smooth as wax. Even more extraordinary was the touch of his hands on his balls and the base of his cock. Strangest of all was the sliding sensation of hairless balls against hairless thighs. Craig had never imagined that. Flesh more sensitive and alive than he had ever felt it before....

Ready now, he stands in the soft candle glow and dares to look at his reflection.

Craig draws in a sharp, gasping breath. He flushes with excitement, with embarrassment, imagining the body before him on display, his secret exposed to hungry, feverish eyes. It is just as he expected. There is something beautiful about his utter nudity, the way each muscle stands out as clearly defined as a statue's. And something lewd, blatantly alluring, especially between his legs. Beneath his navel, the muscles curve downward in a smooth delta of flesh converging abruptly and nakedly into his cock and the balls that hang below. Everything exposed, nothing concealed. His penis and testicles somehow look larger, stripped of their natural covering. Nude. Vulnerable. On display. Craig stares at the shaved muscleboy in the mirror and his cock stands up hard as rubber.

His outfit for the evening is already laid out and ready on the dresser. Tonight he goes all the way.

He fits the dog collar around his neck. Snaps the cock ring around his genitals. He pauses for a moment, stopped cold by the vision. Muscleboy in a dog collar. Shaved cock and balls harnessed by leather, pushing out plump and smooth between his thighs. Can he really show this to another man? Show him loud and clear what he is, what he wants?

Craig takes a deep breath. Tonight. No turning back.

He slips into his leather chaps. The inner lining glides against his oiled flesh. Every sensation is new, every touch against his skin is powerful and acute. He glances down. Though the chaps' snapped-on rear panel covers his ass, his cock and balls hang smooth and swollen from the open crotch, a fistful of naked need. He snaps the codpiece in place and steps into his boots.

Next is the black ciré tank top. The neckline is cut very deep, so low that it dips below his pectorals, exposing them completely. The fleshy, pumped-up wedges of muscle hang over the hem, putting his nipples on display, accentuating the dog collar. Craig blushes, staring at his reflection. Muscleboy with a big, oil-slicked chest, flaunting his tits.

He pulls on his leather jacket. The night isn't chilly, he doesn't really need it. The coat is a cop-out, he knows that. But to go out on the street wearing only the dog collar and the scoop-necked shirt would overstep even his most blatant fantasy.

He slides his wallet into his jacket pocket, then reaches for his keys, hanging them, after a final moment of hesitation, from his right hip. He picks up a handful of rubbers and stuffs them into his coat pocket. He takes a final look in the mirror, takes a deep breath, and even manages a crooked smile at his own audacity. Now he is ready to go.

Their eye contact is almost immediate, from the moment Craig pushes through the heavy leather curtains and steps into the crowded bar. Across a rippling sea of black leather, he sees the man seated at a corner stool, a drink in his hand. The shiny black brim of his cap conceals his eyes. Then the man looks up, staring straight at him. His features are broad and handsome, with a strong, wide jaw and a thick black mustache. Something in the man's eyes makes him feel already naked and exposed, as if the man can see through the camouflage of the jacket, can penetrate the codpiece of his leather chaps.

For the next half hour, Craig wanders through the crowded bar, pretending to shift his interest casually from face to face, but he keeps one eye on the man and his movements. For a while the man sits alone, nursing his drink, then a few friends come over and join him. They talk and laugh. The man breaks away and moves through the crowd. He seems unaware of Craig, never looking back when Craig darts a quick glance in his direction.

Suddenly Craig loses sight of him. He scans the bar and sees the man nowhere. He steps into the crowd, searching the faces. He circles the bar twice. The man is gone. Craig steps back into an uncrowded corner where he can be alone for a moment.

Then he feels a hand on his shoulder, and he knows.

"You look good tonight."

Craig looks up over his shoulder. The man is tall, looming behind him. His face is lit from above by pale orange light, casting his eyes in shadow, glancing over his smooth, broad lips. Craig's mouth goes dry. "Thanks," he says.

The man circles around him. His movements are casual, but his sheer size backs Craig against the wall. The man is dressed in full leather, from cap to boots. His jacket is unzipped to reveal the deep cleavage between his hard pectorals, matted with swirls of crisp black hair. A pair of handcuffs hangs from his belt, along with a pair of tit-clamps connected by a thin silver chain, and a second length of chain, long and heavy like a leash. The codpiece between his legs bulges outward, heavy and full.

The man smiles faintly. "I've noticed you in here before, kid, but never like this. The leather, I mean. Smells new. You just buy it?" The man looks him up and down. Craig feels a sudden trickle of sweat beneath his arms and legs.

"No, I've had it for a while. But I've never..."

"Never worn it on the street?"

Craig nods, blushing.

The man's faint smile is both reassuring and cool. "You look real good in it. Of course, you look good in jeans and a T-shirt, too. You work out." A statement, not a question, but Craig nods in answer.

"It's hot tonight. You must be pretty sweaty under that jacket. Why don't you unzip it? As I remember, you've got a nice set of tits under there. Shame to keep 'em covered." The man is coming on to him now, his voice still casual but laced with sex. He grabs the zipper at Craig's throat.

Craig reaches up, murmuring a quiet "No." Suddenly he is embarrassed, not yet ready. The man firmly brushes his hand aside and pulls down on the zipper.

He sees the collar first and nods knowingly. Then the expanse of bare flesh as the zipper descends, exposing Craig's chest. He purses his lips, then slips his hands inside the open jacket and onto Craig's bare pecs, cupping the smooth, pumped-up muscles, finding the nipples and gently squeezing them between his forefingers and thumbs. Craig stiffens at first, glancing to each side, realizing that others can see. But the subservient streak rises in him, as if it were being drawn to the surface by the man's fingers pulling on his nipples.

"You like that, don't you?"

"Yes." Craig hisses the word as the man tightens his grip.

"Yeah. Nice, accessible nipples. That why you wore this shirt—so your big smooth tits would be available for me to play with?"

"Yes." Craig bites his lip and flushes.

"So get this jacket out of the way. Go on, take it off."

Craig hesitates, looking nervously around the bar. The man saws his fingernails into the nipples and gives them a twist. His voice is low and hard. "Take off your jacket, kid. Let all the men get a good look at those big shiny tits."

Craig closes his eyes and shrugs the jacket from his shoulders, letting it fall onto the stool behind him. He slips backward, but the man keeps him on his feet, holding him up by his nipples. The man pulls on his tits, testing their elasticity, stretching the fleshy nubs away from the hard muscle beneath. Craig gasps in pain and pleasure.

The man nods and releases him. He fondles the plump pectorals for a moment, cupping them in his hands. "Good. Now go check your coat. And bring me a beer on your way back."

Craig lowers his eyes. His nipples are swollen and tingling from the man's touch. His face is hot. He steps past the man and heads for the coat check.

He keeps his face lowered as he crosses the bar, but he can glimpse the heads that turn in his direction as he walks by, catch fragments of reaction. *Hey, nice tits, boy—like to chew on those—taking your pecs for a walk, kid?* The big man at the coat check window gives him a long, wolfish look as he hands over his jacket. Craig stares down at his chest, at the two sleek, blushing mounds hanging over the hem of the shirt, and his nipples, throbbing and erect from the man's abuse. The big man returns with his check token, a hard square of cardboard. He reaches out and flicks it against one nipple. Craig stands passively, and the man flicks the token against the other nipple with a soft, knowing laugh. "Here, doggy," he says, and pushes the token between Craig's lips.

Craig blushes and takes the token from his mouth. The

man laughs. "Don't worry, kid. Dressed like that, you'll get fed tonight." A group of nearby leathermen take in the joke, snickering as Craig turns and heads for the bar. He walks in a haze, his body hot, his cock stirring in his pants. Exposed. On display.

The bartender is notoriously handsome, a huge, muscular Italian in a white tank top with spiked leather bands around his big biceps. He has never paid any attention to Craig before, but tonight he gives him a long look as he approaches, staring blatantly at his naked chest.

Craig orders the beer and pays. The bartender returns with his change. Craig leaves a dollar behind, but the man slides it back. "I think I like these tips better." He reaches out and gives both nipples a pinch, then tugs at them with his fingernails. Craig's face and chest are burning hot. He turns and hurries back.

The man sits in the corner with an empty stool at his side. He pats the black leather seat as he accepts the beer. Craig sits beside him in silence. Occasionally the man reaches over and touches the frosty glass against his nipples, watching as Craig purses his lips and gasps. The cold touch makes his nipples stand up hard and erect. The man places his hand on Craig's thigh and slowly slips it beneath the codpiece, sliding his fingers between the snaps.

The groping hand touches his cock. Craig is hard. The man nods in approval. Then his fingers explore Craig's crotch, gliding over the smooth, denuded flesh. Craig feels the man's eyes on his face, staring hard.

"You're shaved down there, aren't you? You do it yourself?"

Craig nods.

"Shave your legs, too?"

"Yes, sir."

"Mmm. And your hole? You got a nice, hairless hole between your legs?"

"Yes, sir."

"Good. I like my boys smooth. Come with me, kid."

The man stands. Craig follows him through the crowd, to the far side of the bar. They step through a narrow doorway.

The leather shop is a tiny, cramped room with a glass counter and pegboard walls. Hanging on the walls are paddles, dog collars, restraints. Beneath the glass counter are dildos wrapped in plastic.

"Let me see that one," the man says. The boy behind the counter, staring at Craig's chest, hands the man a short, thick butt plug with leather straps. The man holds it in front of Craig's face, brushing the blunt tip against his lips. "Nice size? Or is this one too small for you?" Craig stands stock-still, blushing furiously.

The man asks to see another, and the salesboy hands him a thicker, larger tool, cock-shaped but with a tapered base and handle to keep it inside. He bats it against Craig's ass, smiling faintly. "I'll take both," he says. Then he laughs softly, tugging at one of Craig's nipples. "Or maybe you'll take 'em, huh, kid?"

They leave the shop, the man carrying the dildos and a small pack of lube in a black bag. "Head for the john," he growls, pushing Craig in front of him.

The bathroom is dark, lit by red lights, and unoccupied. The man pushes Craig roughly down the aisle to the last stall and inside, closing the door behind him. Craig turns to face him, alarmed at the man's sudden roughness, but the man spins him around, pulling his arms behind his back. Suddenly the handcuffs are around his wrists, cinching them tight.

"What are you—"

"Just shut up and enjoy it," the man growls. "I'm gonna give you what you want. Shy little muscleboy, coming in here in his jeans and T-shirt. So you finally got up your nerve to wear your leather. I bet you shaved your crotch for the first time tonight, too. Didn't you?"

"Yes," Craig whispers.

"I know what you are. A little show-off, coming in here with your big, smooth tits hanging out. Cocktease. Yeah, you want the guys to stare, don't you? But you're just a little shy, huh? Too much of a pussy to really do it right. So I'm gonna help you out."

The man pushes him down, forcing him to bend at the waist until his face is in the toilet bowl, his ass pointing up. The man unsnaps the rear panel of the chaps and pulls it down, and Craig feels the man's hands on his naked ass.

"Pretty butt, kid. Hard, smooth, and hairless." The man scoops out some lube and slaps it against Craig's asshole, then begins to work his middle finger inside. Craig bolts and tries to stand, but the man forces him down. Suddenly the finger is all the way inside him, twisting and stretching the hole, pressing on his prostate. Craig gradually relaxes, and the man adds his fore-finger, sawing them in and out, finger-fucking his hole.

The man pulls out, and then Craig feels something else at his ass, smooth and blunt. Craig remembers the butt plug, but as it enters him, he realizes the shaft is bigger than that. The man is pushing the dildo up his ass.

Craig moans as the rubber shaft penetrates him and slides relentlessly inward, until the lips of his hole slip down over the tapered end and press against the flat base. The whole thing is lodged inside him, hard and thick.

The man snaps the leather flap back in place and pulls him up by his shoulders. Standing makes the dildo straighten inside him and press heavily against his prostate. Craig whimpers and his cock throbs inside his codpiece.

The man spins him around. He smirks. "You look uncomfortable, kid. That dildo feel a little too big up your ass? Let me give you something to distract you." He takes the tit-clamps from his belt and snaps them onto Craig's nipples. The metal teeth bite into the tender flesh. The thin connecting chain dips between his pecs.

Craig writhes and moans. "Please—"

"And I can see I'm gonna have to shut you up." The man pokes the smaller butt plug against his lips. Craig draws back, but the man grabs his hair. "Open wide, boy." He forces the plug against Craig's mouth, forcing him to open. The plug slides inside, and Craig's lips close around the narrow base. The man pulls the straps around his head and ties them in a knot. The leather pulls hard against the corners of his mouth.

"There. And just to make sure you keep your place..." The man attaches the heavy chain to the dog collar around Craig's neck, gripping the other end in his fist. He opens the door to the stall and tugs on the leash.

Two men are pissing at the trough. They look up in surprise, then narrow their eyes in excitement. The man stops before a full-length mirror. "Take a good look at yourself, kid."

Craig stares at his reflection under the dim red light. Muscleboy in tight leather chaps and a scoop-neck shirt. Arms handcuffed behind his back, making his big shaved pecs stand out. Nipples clamped. Mouth stuffed with a thick rubber butt plug. Dog collar around his throat, being led by his Master on a leash. The dildo feels huge in his ass. His cock is rock hard, straining against the codpiece, clearly outlined inside the supple leather.

"I'm gonna show you off, boy. Give the guys a good look. This is how they're all gonna see you, just like this. Too bad it's not legal to show 'em what's in your pants. But I'll make sure they all know you shaved your crotch for me." The man gives a hard tug on the leash. "Come on, kid."

The man leads him through the bar, tugging on the leash whenever Craig hesitates or falls too far behind. The crowd parts to make way for them. Craig can feel them watching—blatant stares as brutal as a slap, eyes that rake over his body like fingernails. The man is showing him off, putting him through his paces.

They circle the bar, returning to the empty corner where they met. The man settles himself on a stool and pulls Craig close, angling the leash downward, forcing him to bend and then drop to his knees. The man yanks on the leash, until Craig is where he wants him—kneeling at the man's feet, knees apart, crotch pressed against the man's leg, face buried between the man's thighs. The man's erection is a solid ridge outlined within the thin leather of his codpiece. Craig presses his mouth against the bulge and feels its warm pulse against his lips.

His crotch is hooked on the man's boot. The man flexes his foot, pressing the square toe against Craig's ass, pushing at the base of the dildo, sliding the concealed rubber shaft in and out of Craig's hole with a slow, steady rhythm. Craig gasps and gurgles around the butt plug in his mouth. The man chuckles and pulls Craig's face deeper into his hugely packed crotch, reaches down to run his fingertip over the boy's stretched lips. With his other hand he pulls at the thin chain connecting the tit-clamps, pulling Craig's nipples into sharp points.

The heat slowly gathers, and then comes together all at once. The sensations in his ass and nipples, the man controlling him, the heat of the man's leather-covered cock against his face, his own hard cock hunching the man's leg like a dog, the knowledge that every man in the bar is watching—Craig suddenly goes stiff, shuddering and jerking like a puppet. He hears the man laughing above him as he shoots in his pants, writhing uncontrollably against the man's leg. His asshole spasms in time with his cock, clenching against the thick dildo that still moves relentlessly inside him. He gasps for breath and groans against the plug in his mouth.

Then he crashes. Craig blushes bright red. The clamps on his nipples suddenly turn from pleasure to pain, and the dildo is too much to take. He twists against the handcuffs binding his arms, strains against the leash at his throat, desperate to escape. But the man holds him in place. Craig is helpless. Completely vulnerable. Exposed.

"I'm not through with you yet, you little cocktease. Not by a long shot." The man stands and pulls him to his feet. Craig's legs are wobbly; he follows stumbling as the man walks him across the bar, to a small elevated platform. The regulars call it the auction block. Craig has seen men stand here before, slaves put on display by their masters. His climax has subsided; the heat is gone, the fantasy is over, but the man still controls him. Mouth plugged and hands bound, he has no choice.

His skin prickles with embarrassment as the man pulls him up onto the leather-padded stage, forcing him to face the crowd. The man whispers in his ear. "They all know you now. They all saw the ride you took on my leg, watched you shoot in your pants. This is the way they'll remember you. Every time you step in this bar, they'll know who you are. What you are. What you want, slaveboy. Now I'm gonna go tell my buddies about that shaved crotch of yours."

And then the man is gone, leaving him alone on the block. Craig stands with his head bowed, glancing furtively into the crowd. Faces are turned in his direction. The man is at the bar, having another beer, talking with a group of friends. They look in his direction and laugh, stare, and rub their crotches.

His nipples ache. The handcuffs cut into his wrists and pull at his shoulders, cramping them. His cock and balls are slick inside the codpiece, swimming in his own cum. And then, very slowly, he begins to stiffen again. This is what he wanted. To be seen and desired. To have his secrets bared, even against his will. Suddenly he imagines himself completely naked. His cock strains against the codpiece, fully erect again, blotting out all his inhibitions. He slowly begins to move his hips, squeezing his ass around the dildo embedded in his bowels. The fantasy is ecstatic. Craig is a nude slaveboy on the block, shaved, bound and gagged, penetrated, and put on exhibit by his master.

Hours seem to pass, but the heat never subsides. He glances up, and the faces change, but they are always watching him, the hungry eyes stroking and caressing him, prodding him on.

"You like this, don't you?" The man is behind him, whispering into his ear, his hand reclaiming the leash and jerking his head back.

Craig can only groan against the plug in his mouth.

"You little cocktease." The man spins him around and pulls him off the block. He holds Craig's coat in one hand, the leash in the other. "Come on, muscleboy. I'm gonna take you for a ride on the back of my chopper. Show you off to the whole city."

As the bartender announces last call, the man pulls him stumbling through the heavy leather curtains that drape the front entrance, leading him onto the sidewalk and into the night. Exhausted. Exhilarated. Exposed.

THE ENGLISH

Shaun Levin

The master is wearing a leather jacket, unzipped, no shirt or vest. His chest hair is thick and dark, the odd strand of white hair visible to anyone who's standing close to him, which the slave is not. The master is framed in the doorway, dim light from inside the house around him, the autumn night air cool against his skin. The slave can see the master's leather trousers are as tight as he'd said they'd be. The slave has done what the master ordered and is standing naked on the doorstep, hugging his chest against the cold. His clothes are at the entrance gate in a clay urn, which the master uses for just that purpose, and for leaving front-door keys when friends come to stay.

"Hello, boy," the master says.

The slave's accent, when he replies, is Mediterranean.

The master stands aside to let the boy in. He detects Davidoff's Cool Water and fresh sweat; he has never been a fan of body odors. The slave has tight brown curls and the kind of smooth skin that drops of water roll off. The master would like to touch him, run the tips of his fingers along the boy's back, but he must savor this anticipation. The master loves a sense of menace, that combination of decorum and violence. An hour and ten minutes he'd waited for the slave, which had given him time to sort out the lighting, to shadow and spotlight appropriately, to do forty-three push-ups—one for each year, and one for good luck—to accentuate his biceps, and then a warm shower, not too hot. Hot showers made it harder to come.

"Your house it is nice," the slave says.

"I like it," says the master.

The slave likes rich men, especially rich Englishmen; they're always very perverse, which is why he has moved to London. Athens didn't have that kind of person. The master's house is the biggest he's seen so far. From the hallway the slave can make out a living room with a fire burning, a kitchen that looks clean and unused, a staircase going up and another, broader one, all wood, going down. He catches the glimpse of a library. The garden at the back is lit up from the ground—the master follows the slave's gaze—spotlights nestling amongst the apple and maple trees, a burkwood tree, a rosemary bush. The slave knew some rich men in Athens, but they always became very boring and wanted to take care of him. And he knew some army officers who would speak to him like he was a new recruit. The slave had managed to get himself discharged at eighteen, so he definitely wasn't going to take that kind of talk at twenty-three, *efharisto* very much.

"You find it all right?" the master says.

"Yes," the slave says.

"Yes what, boy?" the master says.

"Yes, Master," the slave says.

He's glad he agreed to come to the master's house; he wants to get to know different parts of London, and the master is tall and broad and hairy like he said on his profile, so that when he feels the man's fingers on his spine, from his nape to the curve in his lower back, ushering him farther inside, the slave is immediately hard. He can feel the warmth from the fire.

"Yes, *Sir,*" the master says. "It's yes, *Sir,*" and presses his chest to the boy's back.

"Yes, Sir," the slave says. "I sorry, Sir."

In the living room, the master faces his slave; he hugs him and cups the boy's balls in his palm. The balls are tight and covered in a soft fuzz. *Like kiwi fruit,* the master thinks. He grips the back of the boy's head with his other hand and sticks his tongue down his throat, tightens his grip on the boy's balls, whispers "walk" against his ear.

The boy is about five eleven, a good two inches shorter than the master; he is slim and smooth, like he said he'd be. The master likes honesty. There's fear or naïveté in a man compelled to tell the truth. The master thinks it's healthier to fabricate, to stretch the truth, play games—especially with men who are boys.

"Get down," the master says.

"Yes, Sir," the slave says, sinking to his knees, relieved they can now begin.

"Lick my boots," the master says.

"Boots?" the boy says.

"Boots," the master says, and steps back from the slave to point to his own feet.

"Ah," the slave says. "Shoes."

"Lick," the master says.

The slave kisses the master's boots. He hugs the master's leg as if it were a tree trunk, strokes the leather trousers as he brings his lips to the boot.

The master has thick calf muscles, from cycling and triathlon, from the years when he had more energy than he knew what to do with. He still keeps fit: three times a week at the gym; the occasional jog in the park; long walks in the countryside every other weekend. He likes it when a slave appreciates his body, a body he turns himself on with when he stands in front of the bathroom mirror and pinches his nipple and jerks off into the sink.

"Lick," the master says.

"I lick very much," the slave says, looking up at his master like a dog.

"No," the master says, and lifts the boy to his feet. He is light and soft and yielding. "Lick."

And he runs his tongue along the boy's neck, so smooth, skin that tastes of baby oil. The master could fuck him right there and then, but he knows he must draw this out, get ultimate pleasure from his cute slaveboy, the boy who traveled from Vauxhall to Highgate to do just this. Besides, these days, it takes the master longer to build up a second load, and he'd already come once while chatting to the slave in the chatroom, shooting onto his stomach while he described to the boy how he'd tie him up and fuck his cunt when he came over.

"See," he says to the slave. "Lick," and he points to his tongue.

The slave loves having his neck licked, loves being in the arms of a big man, the hairier the better. He'll do just about anything to be with a big, hairy man, a man into whose shadow he can disappear. But he will not, how you say, *lick* the boots. He doesn't care if they're new or not. He's not having shoe polish in his mouth. This was not something he'd ever had to deal with in Greece. Most of the time it was too hot for this kind of stuff; you had to turn on the air-conditioning if you wanted to wear leather.

"I lick your cock," the slave says.

"You're fucking right you will," the master says.

His own words excite him, pump blood into his cock. To call his boy a pussy, to get his slave to milk his tits, to make the boy his to do with what he wishes: the master gets hard very quickly when the opportunity to degrade presents itself. Sometimes this scares him, though he's constantly surprised by the number of men who will take orders from him. Like this Mediterranean boy whose face is nuzzling in his chest. So pliant in his arms is the boy, the master knows he will let him do anything. He's pleased he had the time to shower. He feels ready. The master takes off his jacket, grabs the back of the boy's head and presses his face onto his nipple.

"Suck," he tells the slave.

"Yes, Sir," the slave says.

"Harder," the master says.

The slave takes his mouth off the master's nipple.

"Yes, Sir," he says, and puts his mouth back on again.

"Come on, work it, baby," the master says. "Harder."

The slave loves to bring pleasure to big men, and from the sounds the master is making, he is liking what the slave is doing. The boy pinches the other nipple with the tips of his fingers, and rubs his own cock against the master's leg, the sensation of the leather against his shaft bringing a tingle to his body that he can feel all the way to his teeth. Once he and his friend Nikos talked about leather and what it was about it that got them so excited. Nikos said it was genetic, from when we all wore animal skins. The slave thought it might have something to do with life and death, the smell of a corpse on a breathing man's skin. The slave is now a masseur by profession. He is doing a course in holistic methods at City and Islington College.

The master starts to undo his own trousers, to let the slave know that soon he will have to suck cock. The master goes weak when someone's working on his tits, it confuses him, and at moments like this he could kneel down on all fours and get fucked from behind. It's been years since that has happened, since anyone's wanted to fuck him. The master's been fucked before. He is not an unbending man. But at moments like this, when ecstasy threatens to undermine the distinction between top and bottom, he has to remind himself who the master is.

"You ready to suck cock?" he says.

He thinks of cunt and pussy and the boy on his back spreading the cheeks of his arse so that his hole is like a twat, so that when the slave tries to help him open his trousers, he slaps the boy's hands away. He wants to do this on his own, to have his boy stand back and watch. He knows the effect it has on them when his trousers are unzipped and his long thick cut cock is slowly lifted out into the light.

"Yeow," the slave says.

"Can you take this, boy?" the master says.

"Yes, please, Master, Sir," the slave says.

He has never seen cock this size. Back in Athens everyone seemed to have the same fifteen centimeters, if not smaller.

"Now, suck it," the master says.

"Yes, please," the slave says.

"Slowly," says the master. "Just the head first."

The slave is happy. Get him on his knees, feed him cock, and he's in pig heaven. He moves slowly, maybe too slowly, hoping the master will slap his face with his cock. He likes to have a huge cock smacked against his cheek. Like this.

"Thank you, Sir," he says.

"Suck it," the master says.

The master reproaches himself for duplication; he must be

careful not to give the same orders twice. It's a sign of laziness. That kind of repetition is pornographic.

"Put your pussy lips around my fat cock," he says. "Your fucking faggot lips on this piece of meat."

The slave's mouth is wet and soft and the master thinks about the erotic power of adjectives as he holds on to the back of the boy's head and gradually shoves his cock down the slave's throat. The slave's hunger is turning him on, the slobbering and sucking sounds, the closing of the eyes, the intense frowning, it could be the Eucharist for all he knew. The master loves to watch a boy on his knees in front of him sucking on his big fat hairy man cock. Without it, who knows what kind of man the master would have become.

"Feed on it," the master says. "Suck the milk."

The slave is having a ball.

The master's not sure where to take it from here, how to get the boy downstairs to the playroom. He could pick him up in his arms and carry him like a bride, or push him off his cock, strap the leash around his neck and walk him on all fours down the stairs. There was a time when he used to do whatever came to mind, when he'd not think before acting, before getting men to comply to his will. At what point, the master asks himself, did I lose my spontaneity? When did I stop being vicious? He knows it has something to do with age and this growing need—as if a great winter were approaching—to hibernate.

"What the fuck do you think you're doing, boy?"

The slave has a finger feeling around in the master's crack. The master lifts his boot and kicks the slave off his cock. The slave falls back and lies on the floor, lifting his head just a fraction, his eyes still lowered, to see what the master's going to do next.

"Are you trying to fuck me, boy?" the master says, immediately sorry he'd said it, afraid his words came across as defensive, concerned that the slave had been reading his thoughts. *Do I sound whiny?* he wondered. "Is that what you're doing, boy?"

"No, Sir."

And it's true. All the slave wanted was to touch the thick hair in the master's arse crack, hoping he'd let him lick his hole. He liked the arseholes of hairy men; it's like they were never fully clean, the sweet taste of shit lingered. The carpet breaks the slave's fall, it is thick and soft; he's never been kicked like that before. The master is standing over him, looking down, with his hard cock sticking out of his trousers like a lever. The master lifts his boot and puts it on the slave's chest.

"Don't fuck with me, boy," the master says.

He keeps his eyes fixed on the boy's, and his voice is a whisper. The boy—thank fuck—looks scared.

"Okay, Sir."

"Shut the fuck up, boy," the master says. "No more talk. Shut up."

He puts his boot under the boy's arse and flips him over onto his front. His back is beautiful, and his arse, and his legs. The short dark hairs on the backs of his thighs get thicker around his crack. Everything about the slave's body is perfect. The master feels that rush of sadness and nausea he has come to recognize as envy. He has never loved his own body, especially now that it has become big and covered in hair, as if his body will never again be able to pretend youth and boyishness. He puts his open palms under the boy's waist and lifts his arse into the air. He kneels down behind the boy and places his mouth against the boy's hole. Its smell is delicate and pure; you'd think he never had to shit. The master wants to make his way into the boy, to open him up and disappear into the tight, young, smooth, untroubled body.

The slave moves his hips in circles. The master's silence is confusing him. He doesn't want to do the wrong thing. He doesn't want to be kicked again. He stays on his hands and knees while the master takes off his boots and his leather trousers and presses his chest against the boy's back. The slave can feel the hair rubbing against his skin; it's as exciting as leather. He can feel the master's cock against his crack. He can hear the master tear open a condom and put it on his cock. He knows the master is spitting into his palm and wiping the spit against his hole.

The master enters the boy the way some people enter temples, the way virgins step up to the altar. As he makes his way into the slave's arse, the boy turns to look at him, his curls flopping against his face, and he smiles at the master, his master, the kind of smile the master has seen on the faces of boys who are getting what they want, who have found a man with a cock that makes them feel full. They can let go. They will never have to make another decision, never have to look after themselves. Never again in their whole lives. That's what the master gives.

The master goes through the motions, says the right words, calls the boy names. And the slave loves it, moves his head from side to side, pushes his arse into the master's pelvis, makes whimpering noises, those signs of helplessness and surrender that give the master his sense of purpose. What really takes the master over the edge is when the boy's hole is so loose there's hardly any friction, his arse so soft that the master feels there is nothing to touch his cock. It is all faith and his own imagination, the boy's hunger to be taken, and the master's own desire to give another what he wants.

After they come, they spoon.

The slave and the master both want to say how much they love each other.

"Thank you, Sir," the slave says.

"It's Thomas," the master says.

"Thank you, Thomas," the slave says.

"No need for all this gratitude," the master says.

"I don't know the English so good," the slave says.

"We're a strange bunch," the master says.

"Bunch?" the slave says.

"Your English is fine," the master says.

He's known worse. Moroccan boys he'd had to speak French to, which only made him feel inadequate. A Swede from Amsterdam whose hair the master had to grab to get him to do what he wanted. The Swede—the one and only fucking Swede who couldn't speak English—had followed the master back to London, but the master liked language, liked to order his slaves around, and what's the point of an order if no one carries it out immediately? Orders are like magic words; they're ridiculous if they don't bring the rabbit from the hat or make the coin disappear.

"You have something to drink?" the slave says.

"I could make us some tea," the master says, thinking how to get up from the floor in an elegant way, to move casually as the slave stares at his back, at the folds of skin under his buttocks. When he rises, he will walk to the kitchen, where he will spoon fresh leaves into the teapot while the kettle boils. First he touches the slave's cheek, kisses his forehead.

"Tea, then?" he says.

"Tea is good," the slave says, as he cuddles up to the master. "You have peppermint?"

YUMMY

Bill Brent

It seemed like Sunday evenings were always blustery in SOMA, as if wind were nature's way of shaking any residual haze off the neighborhood's weekend partyers.

Conrad had gone to retrieve a fellow cast member's bracelet, an heirloom she had accidentally worn to last night's show—"guerrilla cabaret," the local alt-weekly had dubbed it—and then left behind. Sometimes Conrad thought that Laura lived in a permanent haze all her own. Such a fun gal to do a show with, though. Her buoyant attitude was infectious, which was good, since it compensated for her ditzy tendencies.

He chased up the stairs, two at a time, giddy and cold, trying to burn off a bit of his own nearly unbearable exuberance. He pressed the access code into the alarm system, and soon he was inside the darkened theater.

Smells: Stale coffee. Sawdust. Printer's ink from the posters and programs. Latex paint-stink. And a subtle, underlying raw stench like piss. No sound but his own slight panting.

He flicked on the meager track lights, their buzz now adding a bass tone to his rhythmic breath as he fumbled to the closetlike dressing rooms, where he spotted Laura's heirloom bracelet on a makeshift plywood makeup table.

He hadn't given in to his sexual urges in quite a few days, and it crossed his mind to relieve himself promptly into the sink. He gave his crotch a squeeze, and it responded with a throb.

He thought better of unzipping, though, and decided he'd wait until he was alone later that night.

In a moment he was back across Folsom Street, headed up Eighth toward Howard. The Sunday paper caught his eye. He'd been so wrapped up in the week's frenzy that he'd not even scanned a paper this week.

He bent over the newspaper rack. Reagan, still focused on SDI rather than AIDS. Same old Star Wars. Same old bullshit. Nothing ever changed. Why bother reading the news at all? At least he was doing something meaningful with his life, he told himself.

And then he looked up, and he saw the man who would change it.

He could see the man's purposeful stride from across the street. Powerful legs clad in leather, a massive, bulging crotch. Then a vest around a broad chest; thick neck, set jaw.

His boots hammered the crosswalk, just moments away. Conrad had seen some meaty leather daddies roaming the shadowy streets and alleys of SOMA, but this one was prime. He glistened from head to toe with power. His eyes glittered with depth and menace. He was Conrad's vague, half-illuminated fantasies sculpted into flesh.

Conrad's stomach leapt in panic and terror. Blood pounded in his ears. Slow-motion tension. There was an awkward instant, then Conrad felt his neck turning his head away from the object of ultimate desire.

His face flushed, bright red. "I'm unworthy," he scolded himself. "This guy could have anyone. *Anyone*.... But he's alone now."

Rebelling against his shyness, he turned his head to watch the receding hulking figure turning his head at exactly the same instant, looking at Conrad's curvaceous ass. Conrad gulped, hard, engulfed by a shivering wave of fear. The leatherman stepped into the nearest doorway as Conrad's hungry eyes followed his figure.

There are two kinds of people in this world: those who leap off cliffs, and those who watch.

Trust your impulse.

Conrad walked into the doorway. The leatherman's eyes burned into his as he opened the flap of his vest to reveal the hugest, most perfect male nipple Conrad had ever seen.

The stranger groaned appreciatively as Conrad chewed his meaty tit. This seemed right to Conrad. What could be more natural than for two horny men, meeting for the first time on Folsom Street, to start making love right there in the street? Or humping like animals? Same difference sometimes.

But then Conrad grew self-conscious, suddenly aware of the cold breeze racing around his ears. He didn't want to be surprised and embarrassed by passersby, but neither did he want to ruin this moment. In his confusion, he smiled into the guy's brutishly rugged face.

"Yummy," he exhaled. "But, um, could we find some place a little less public?" Yet if the guy had responded by stepping into the sidewalk and hauling out his cock, Conrad would have dropped to his knees.

"How much time you got?"

"Uh—about ten minutes."

The hunk smirked. "Well, let's see what we can do in 'ten minutes.' "

He adroitly picked up Conrad by the scruff of his neck, hoisting him off his feet. The man's power, terrifying and awesome, was the sexiest thing Conrad had ever experienced. His half-hard dick sprung to full, surprised attention instantly, as the demigod dragged him, startled, down the nearest alley.

The alley was one of those peculiar little side streets that weave through SOMA like strands in a spiderweb. At the moment, Conrad felt very much like the fly. The leatherman hauled him past the dreary eyes of the homeless men encamped behind the Ozanam shelter. He stopped before one of the miniature-scale Victorian dwellings, penetrated the bars and locks with his keys, pushed Conrad inside, and dumped him immediately into a small, dark front parlor stuffed with a baby grand and shelves crammed with LPs. Sheet-music books climbed precariously toward the ceiling, into the dark.

The deadbolt clicked shut behind him. The dim light snapped on, doing little to banish the gloom. Conrad had to step carefully to avoid toppling the stacks of music placed about the floor. "Nice piano," he croaked. In response, the leatherman pushed him backward with one palm. One slight gesture—more of a shrug, really—forceful enough to send Conrad reeling back. His shoulder blades slapped into a sliding wall panel. Perhaps this guy was a maniac, but Conrad's dick remained hard.

Now the arm reached around him and gathered him toward the meaty lips that crashed into his in a thrilling, invasive tonguelock. Crushed between the wall and the leatherman's sculpted pectorals, Conrad could hardly breathe. He inhaled the arousing blend of beer, leather, and armpit sweat. The bodybuilder plundered Conrad's mouth until he was satisfied that the other man had relaxed a bit. Then he slid open the door in the wall with a fierce tug. Conrad stumbled backward into the bedroom.

"Strip."

Conrad shucked his clothes, placing them into a neatly folded pile on the floor. The canopied bed seemed less a place of rest than a place of restraint, filling as much of the space as the piano had the previous room. Heavy four-by-four timbers full of eye-hooks dominated the room. Hands clasped behind his back, he stood in front of the man, who batted Conrad's erection back and forth between his palms, smirking.

"You've done this before?" he asked.

"A little," Conrad lied.

"So what are you into?"

"I'm willing to try a lot of different things. It's just that—well, I like the idea of being dominated by someone as gorgeous and strong and in command as you. I'm kind of intimidated—quite scared, really—but I like that, I guess."

The guy batted at Conrad's still-raging hard-on. "Get on the bed."

Conrad climbed up onto the elevated mattress. A series of drawers on the underside no doubt contained a lot of the things he'd seen in the kinky store down the block from his apartment. The guy tugged at the corners of the bed, revealing leather wrist and ankle restraints. Conrad was surprised to hear running steps on the ceiling, followed by the arguing voices of kids upstairs, and the scolding, clearly parental voice of a young woman.

The guy followed Conrad's gaze toward the plastered ceiling. "Just ignore them. Make all the noise you want. Stupid little bastards." Conrad looked uncertain and self-conscious. "I'll put on some music, then." Half-expecting a Tchaikovsky concerto, Conrad was a bit surprised when the sinewy, synthesized tones of Depeche Mode snaked their way into the room. He thought of the guys who lived downstairs from him and wondered if Depeche Mode was the unofficial rock band of leathermen everywhere.

"No one has ever tied me up before, and you haven't even told me your name."

"It's Ben."

"Ben Steele," Conrad replied. He felt the sting of Ben's stare. "I saw it printed on the mailbox."

"You're very observant."

"Well, just in case you turn out to be a homicidal maniac, and I have to file a police report." Conrad grinned. Ben grinned back, abruptly flipping Conrad over. He locked Conrad's ankle into a fleecy restraint. The left shortly followed.

Ben approached the head of the bed. "Now, the only other words I want to hear from you are "Yes, Sir" and "Thank you, Sir."

"Yes, Sir." One restraint was on his wrist. "Thank you, Sir." Both were locked securely in place. Conrad emitted an exultant sigh.

Ben's hands squeezed his limber frame, massaging him sadistically. Ben pressed, then slapped, then pummeled Conrad's tender flesh. Slaps began to rain down upon Conrad's butt, soft and sensuous at first, but quickly progressing to hard and stinging. He cried out in pain, then remembered. "Thank you, Sir."

"You like that, do you, boy?"

"Yes, Sir."

The slapping stopped. Conrad heard the leatherman pluck something off a rack along the wall, and then felt the whack of a large leather paddle across his ass.

"OW! Thank you, Sir." The pain splashed bloody red beneath his tightened eyelids.

"Good boy. You can take a lot more than that. And you will."

After a while, the sharpness of the blows seemed to subside, and all Conrad felt was their rhythmic impact to the music's beat. He heard himself screaming, but it wasn't him; that part of his being was disconnected, howling somewhere off in the distance. He truly didn't care about anything except bending to the will of this half-man, half-beast, half-god. His blissed-out math transcended logic.

Too soon, the leatherman unsnapped the restraints and flipped Conrad over, securing just his ankles. Ben tore off the pouch restraining his cock and balls, and everything came tumbling out in a rush. Conrad gulped hard at the size and beauty of Ben's privates, in polished and massively perfect proportion to the rest of the man. Here was a feast.

Ben thrust his crotch rhythmically as his mighty cock grew erect over Conrad's hungry mouth. He seated himself on Conrad's upturned face.

"Play with my tits, boy."

Conrad sucked on the hunky leatherman's tight, massive ball sac. His index fingers snaked skyward to grapple with Ben's stainless steel nipple rings. He felt a surge of warm blood shoot under the leathergod's nuts and into his hardening dick as he tugged on the rings. "Yeah, work my tits, you hungry little ballsucker," Ben growled. "See what you can get for all your hard work. Gonna make me shoot, boy?" The hunk tangled his fingers in Conrad's wavy brown hair and pulled hard, jacking his own hot dick with his other hand. Conrad groaned, his untouched cock throbbing in response to the leatherman's harsh touch.

Conrad nuzzled the nut sac with his nose, splaying his flat, wide tongue across Ben's perineum. He wanted badly to scoop his salivating tongue down deeper, to feast on the delicious, musky warmth of the topman's hole. He was so ready. *Don't,* a voice within him warned. *Mustn't do that anymore.* Conrad groaned in frustration; Ben thought it was lust. No one knew how little cum or precum it would take to infect someone. No one knew anything for certain. Everywhere, quacks promised solutions. And everywhere, people were dying.

Yet what point was there to a life half-lived? What was left if one could not do as he pleased? What if he lived through this, by following what were at best tentative guidelines for sexual conduct—exercising completely unnatural restraint—until a cure was maybe, eventually, found? Would all his friends be dead by then? Would he ever again be able to give himself over fully to passion? Most likely, sex would never be the way it had been before.

"I wanna fuck your face, cocksucker."

"Yes, Sir," he grunted hoarsely. "Um...could you wear a rubber?" *Please don't let him be one of those guys who can't keep a hard-on with a condom on.* The muscleman pulled a plastic square out of a glass on the bedside table. Conrad salivated as Ben worked the stretched-out piece of latex over his lengthy, unusually thick dick. He felt a tug on his scalp as Ben shoved his face into his crotch.

Ptheah! The sharp, bitter taste of latex almost gagged him. Its texture rubbed on Conrad's raw throat, already scratchy from shouting, and now well-stretched by Ben's tremendous girth. Conrad sank into this new, more familiar variation on his submissive role with gusto, and soon Ben was groaning and gasping with zeal.

Ben grunted, yanked his cock out of Conrad's surprised mouth, tore off the rubber, and began whipping his enormous cock with a violent frenzy, slapping it around and jerking it furiously. He sat once again on Conrad's mouth, and this time the boy managed to cram both of the leatherman's enormous sperm-globes into his mouth. He grabbed his own thick, furious cock as he suffocated in delirium under Ben's crushing weight. The pressure of Conrad's mouth encased around his nuts caused Ben to scream in agony and delight, and his quads gripped the boy's ears as he shot long, leaping strands of sperm onto Conrad's chest and stomach. Conrad's own cock spurted forth, its juices crossing and mixing with the leatherman's ropy load.

It took four full minutes for the men to regain their composure.

Ben broke the silence, throwing him a small towel with the Crisco logo embroidered in red on one corner. "So how's that for ten minutes?"

Conrad glanced at the clock. Over an hour had passed. "Well, I've probably missed dinner, but I've never had a better reason for skipping a meal."

"Well, this was a different kind of feeding," the leatherman joked wanly.

"I'd love to see you again sometime when I'm not in a hurry."

"Sure, I'll give you my number," Ben agreed. "I'm very busy with teaching and performing lately, but if it works out...."

Ten minutes later, he was out the door and walking back to the cramped apartment he shared with Laura, her friend Ellen, and his two kittens. He rounded the corner and spotted Laura heading his way. She eyed him suspiciously. "Everything all right?"

"Oh, yeah, sure," Conrad grinned. "Here's your bracelet," he said, handing Laura her treasure.

"What took you so long, then? I'd given up on you."

"It's a long story. I'll tell you later."

They soon arrived at Laura's favorite restaurant in the Mission, renowned for its burritos, not its comfort. They sat on wooden benches; Conrad could hardly keep still as they enjoyed the meal.

Laura regarded him quizzically. He gave her a sheepish smile, wiggling his butt against the bench in a futile attempt to find relief from Ben's bruising.

"Yummy," was all he said.

SALVATION

Alana Noël Voth

Life, like death, came with a bang. With one laced-up black boot, this guy kicked a door open, then barged into a public bathroom, bleeding on the floor.

"Didn't know anyone was in here." The guy held his bleeding hand in front of him. He wore a leather jacket over his bare chest, white with a glimpse of rusty nipple.

The piss spilling from my dick had stopped long before, and I'd been standing at the urinal frozen as a fool. Now I felt myself blink.

The guy walked over and stood behind me. Then he peered over my shoulder. "Nice cock."

"What?" I could smell him, leather and sweat, the blood coming from his knuckles—all like metal-scorched rain. For the first time in months I felt turned on.

"Turn around," the guy said.

"What?" I said again, developing a pattern, although I really wasn't dense, just out of it lately. I fumbled with the fly of my jeans, buttoned up.

"Damn, why'd you do that?"

I felt confused. Maybe I should unbutton again. Maybe I should just get out of there. I turned to face him, not sure what to do, and for a moment we stood inches apart.

He took a couple steps back before shaking his bleeding hand, so blood sprayed a few feet away. I flinched. He noticed.

"Afraid of blood?"

"No," I said, too fast of course.

"Uh huh." The guy had a Sid Vicious–like face if you can imagine a modelesque version of Vicious. Sharp cheekbones, strong chin, and wide lips. His eyes were the color of, what was that, sky through a smudged window? The guy had a wiry build but muscled, skin pale as a bead of jizz. He'd dyed his hair blue with patches of black.

I was medium height and skinny, brown eyes and dirty-blond hair; doable, I guessed. Except I'd felt ready to stand at the urinal all day pissing my life away, so to speak, because Dad was dead. Ever smelled brains on a carpet? I wasn't happy to be witness to his execution. Now I had money to go to college, so I was supposed to go on with my life or some crap like that, except I didn't want to do anything. Except maybe this beautiful guy. *You're a love letter to faggots*, I thought, *a gay boy's effervescent wet dream*. People had told me I had a talent for words, which was how I'd ended up at college—besides insurance money—but so far I hadn't gotten farther than the bathroom.

"I'm Steely Dan," the guy said.

Crazy. No. Fitting, I thought. *Yeah*. I said, "Yeah."

"Got to have balls of steel to be me," he continued.

"Yeah," I said again, then tried not to dwell on the shame of being a chickenshit.

Steely Dan took a step backward, then cupped his balls.

"Balls like you wouldn't believe, baby." I liked how he said *baby* and felt one corner of my mouth tug toward the ceiling. The guy wore rings on three fingers, and one ring was metal. I started to reach for his hand—swollen knuckles pocked by little mouths, jagged remnants of skin like fangs leaking blood—and pulled my hand back.

Steely Dan walked to a sink across the bathroom and held his hand under a stream of water. "Sonofabitch that hurts!" He twisted away from the sink, still shoving his knuckles under the water. His leather jacket had fallen open, which gave me a shot of his nipples, a smooth quivering belly, and hair etching a line down his stomach.

Steely Dan opened his eyes and nailed me. "You should tell me your name before we go any further."

I felt myself smile, full-on this time, and the sensation was like opening the front door to Dad's apartment where we used to live, after not having been there in two months. Sun had spilled through the living room window, making me squint.

"Robbie," I said.

Steely Dan met my eyes in the mirror. "Robbie," he said, "is sexy." He turned off the water then lifted his wet hand to study his knuckles.

I took the opportunity to say, "I'm an English major. Writer, I guess."

"No shit?" Steely Dan looked at me again. "I'm going to be a muse."

"Yeah," I said. *Yeah.* Wouldn't I like to slip my tongue through his buttcheeks, part the halves, find me a center to slicker up before I put my cock in there and fucked him? Wouldn't it be great to fuck my nightmares away? Spurt a rainbow of angst-riddled jizz straight up this beautiful guy's ass where *Peace be with you, and also with you.* Dad used to bring women home and fuck them. Last time, after the headboard had stopped slamming the wall, I'd heard screaming threats. "I'll fucking kill you!"

I blocked the sound in my head now, concentrated on Steely Dan as he gazed in a mirror over the sink. Blue hair curled around his pristine ears; more curls covered the collar of his leather jacket. When he moved his arm, a nipple became visible again. Wouldn't I just like to smear that dollop like a dab of blood? Fuck. What was wrong with me? Steely Dan leaned forward and blew a squall of breath at the mirror. Maybe I should carry on with my day. Except why? I'd been planning to stay in the bathroom indefinitely. Steely Dan walked over and held his wounded hand out. "Want to bandage me up, make it better?"

The gun blast had smelled like fire. I'd smelled cooked flesh. *Dad?* My voice had dropped to nothing, like his body to the floor. I'd stared at the blood.

"Hey, it's just a cut," Steely Dan said.

I tried to back away, but he grabbed my face. "What is it?"

"Nothing." Tears pushed at the backs of my eyes.

He let go. Blood had oozed through his split knuckles again. He dabbed his wounds with his tongue. Then he said, "Ever taste blood before?"

"No." I shook my head. As I'd knelt at the edge of a circle of brain stew, I'd had this urge to stick a finger in Dad's blood and taste it, didn't know why. Because I'd suffered a shock, my therapist had said. I'd fled the scene. When I'd come back, I'd puked for a month—at the funeral, in the shrink's office, my own fucking bed. Shame was like seasickness.

"Robbie," Steely Dan said, "what's going on with you? Just tell me."

It made me shiver. I managed to meet his eyes. "Nothing," I said too quickly.

"Uh huh." Steely Dan looked again at his bleeding knuckles.

"How'd you do that?" I asked. Anything to not answer his question.

"Hit a guy."

"Really?" Breath burst through my lips. "Why?"

"He didn't like my shirt."

"What shirt?"

"The one I had on earlier. It said *Sorry Girls, I Suck Dick.*"

"Really?" I started to laugh, and then my eyes watered.

"Yeah," he said.

"Fuck, that's..." I looked at him. "You've got balls," I said.

Steely Dan winked at me. "What did I tell you?"

I swallowed. "Yeah, right. Where's the shirt now?"

"Shoved it through the prick's teeth after I knocked him down."

"Fuck," I said again. I was impressed. Yeah, I was.

"You going to tell me what's bothering you?" Steely Dan said.

"I don't know. It's just...I'm fucked in the head right now."

"Like how?"

Just say it. Ready? Now. "My dad was murdered."

"Shit," Steely Dan said.

"And...I was there. I watched this bitch shoot my dad in the head."

"Jesus Christ," Steely Dan said. "Come here." He took hold of my head, then pulled me forward. He kissed me, and the kiss was like a punctuated moment in a movie, first kiss of a soulful porn. The physical sensation, our proximity, the taste of his spit, all of it overwhelmed me, and I tore into his mouth with my tongue until he pulled back and said, "Okay, okay," into the cavern of my mouth.

"I don't want to stop," I said, then kissed him some more

before shoving my hands under his jacket and reaching around so I felt heat and moisture on his skin from the weight of the leather. He pressed me to a wall. I made a sound like "umph." His cock pressed through his pants, against mine. Stacked. We breathed against each other. He had me pinned by the shoulders. I looked for the blood on me from his hand. Steely Dan grabbed my face. "Look at me." He moved his crotch across mine. I felt precum ooze from my cockhead, and I closed my eyes, then pushed my face in his neck. I bit his leather collar between my teeth, then pushed his jacket open so I could slide my hands over his skin; found a nipple, then thumbed it with my nail. We kissed again. I smelled leather and skin. Heat all around. With one hand pushed under his jacket, I found the seat of his pants, then slipped my hand in his back pocket and grabbed his ass. We switched places. Steely Dan against the wall. I worked his belt buckle open. Finally his cock sprung from his pants, hefty and full. I touched the slit and teased jizz out. Sharp, solid hip bones jutted above the waist of his jeans. I worked my hand inside his pants, behind him to his ass, then slipped a finger through his cheeks to find his hole. Sticky sponge. I lubed him with his own precum. Worked my finger in a bit at a time. My cock pounded with blood.

"Turn around," I said. He did. Round alabaster ass. Right there, shiny dime of skin across his tailbone where I touched him. Steely Dan held his hands on either side of him, against the wall. I lifted my eyes and saw a trickle from his bruised hand again.

"Blood," I said.

He turned around, jarred me. "Sonofabitch."

"Let me see," I said. No running away now. I took his hand and felt the curve of his fingers, warmth coming from the center of his palm, and then he hooked a leg around my waist and pulled me to him before kissing my throat. With his free hand he opened my fly, then jerked me off. I was going to come. I told him so. "Go ahead," he said. I lifted his hand to my lips.

SOUTHERN GOTHIC

Shane Allison

For a minute there, I didn't think he was going to show. Thought I would miss him if I parked at Myers Park instead of the Korean War Memorial like we planned. I woke up that morning with him on the brain. My dick ached to the thought of him, but that was only because it was full with piss. I hoped he would approve of me, wondered if he looked like the man he described in his ad. Pondered if he was really older or younger than the thirty-seven years he gave. Wanted him to be black-haired 'cause I'm a cocksucker for brunets. When he emailed to inform me that his friends had left dinner early but figured that his message would not reach me until the next day, I knew he was in the mood, knew right then he wanted to fuck. Made up his mind days ago that I was the one he wanted.

We decided to meet earlier than the time we'd set. Didn't know how much I could take of walking through the day completely hard. He was early by twenty minutes. My heart went haywire when I saw his black Volvo station wagon descending down Circle Street, curling into the vacant lot where I waited. Was anxious as hell to see him in the flesh after days of corresponding through emails. It was so damn hot that day. The sweat had long since started to roll down my face. I had not planned on waiting long. Had he been a minute late I was going to leave. He wasn't what I imagined. Not brunet, but bald. No hair at all. Prayed he would like me even if I hadn't shaved in days. Hoped he would not find me too fat to fuck. We sat awkwardly in the lot, taking those short pauses I hate, between our conversations about nothing at all.

"So what do you wanna do?" I asked.

"You wanna follow me back to the scary house?"

"Sure," I stated.

I was hot on his ass as he barreled up past gravel lots in the park, empty tennis courts and playgrounds.

Scary house? What the hell did he mean by that? He had eyes that wouldn't wait: hazel. Cherry red lips. Not a slit of a mouth like most white dudes. He reminded me of an actor I've seen, I can't think of who. I followed him as we came to a narrow road lined with azalea bushes. The yard was overgrown with thick grass. I found it peculiar that he was wearing a long-sleeved black shirt, as hot as it was out there on that August afternoon. He made me sweat just looking at him. I wondered what lay beneath his storm gray trousers. He introduced himself to me. Finally, a real name I could put to that movie-star face other than *Southern Gothic.* As we made our way up the steps of the old and beautiful house, my dick twitched nervously in my jeans.

"Would you like something to drink?" he asked. "I have Gatorade, carbonated water...."

I settled on Gatorade even though I don't much care for the stuff. I secretly desired something stronger: a martini, a vodka tonic. Hadn't had a drink since my wild nights in those Westside, New York bars on Christopher Street. He poured the juice in a jelly-jar glass and filled his wineglass with rum. We sat on the yellow vintage sofa. I admired the spacious living room, the matching recliners. I asked him about the family picture that sat on the mantel.

"Those are the people I'm house-sitting for," he said.

We spoke of the difficulties of meeting men in Tallahassee, how they play games, how they lie through their teeth. Turned out that we were both natives of the capital city. I went to Rickards High on the south side while he attended lily-white Florida High on the north. I talked of attending grad school in New York and how easy those Big Apple boys are up there. He spoke of the fetish bars in Atlanta. Leather-clad studs with tit-clamps on their nipples. Oh, the glamorous life we lead. We sipped our drinks, sat there like two nervous schoolboys.

Before he dismissed himself for more booze, he leaned in and laid one on me. His lips felt like cotton. His bubble-gum tongue wormed its way throughout my mouth, under my teeth. He was just like all the rest. Not much for finesse. I slipped a hand around his bald head and pressed him, like a lover, into me. His eyes were closed like they do it on the daytime soaps. I watched him with two eyes that were open slightly. As he refilled his wineglass, I kicked off my Sauconys. I watched his red mouth move as he unfastened the buttons from that pitch black shirt. I didn't pay much attention to the words tumbling out. I was a nervous mess, hoping I would be able to live up to the things I had told him in countless emails. He pulled that shirt off, and I saw white shoulders and a black tee with holes torn out that exposed a leather harness. It all made sense to me. *Southern Gothic.* I'd never been with a goth guy but I'm up for whatever. Our kisses were wet and messy as he fussed with the buttons on my plaid shirt with the bleach spot above the pocket, the shirt I hate 'cause it makes me look fat. We couldn't keep our hands off one another's chests and dicks. I stepped out of my jeans and folded them over the armrest of the couch. I was wearing nothing but tube socks. I covered up, crossed my arms over myself.

"What's wrong?" he asked.

"I hate my body."

He gently pulled my arms down from my chest. I looked to the mint-green carpet, embarrassed.

"I like guys with a little meat on their bones," he said, like that would make me feel less like wanting to cut myself out of this body.

"I'll be right back," he told me. Wondered what he had in mind; if he was gonna come out with a knife to carve my ass. I couldn't help but think the worst. He returned with a collar, a leather-studded thing on the end of a chainlike leash. I'd told him I was kinky. He handed it to me to hold as he yanked his slacks down from his bare ass. He left on the torn tee, the boots with a fucking multitude of buckles. I took the studded collar and buckled it around his goose-bumped neck.

"Not so tight," he told me.

"Sorry." I loosened it at the third or so hole. I took hold of the leash and tugged it delicately.

"Get on your knees."

"Yes, Sir," he said.

He kneeled into the cushions of the sofa. His goth white ass awaited the pleasures I had to give. I made my way between his bent legs and those shiny, black boots. He had the perfect butt. There's nothing better than the asses of white boys. I parted him. He was pink and clean back there, just like he said. I wasted no time and began to eat him alive. Licking, soaking, slurping.

I yanked at the chain, causing the collar to tighten around his jugular.

"You like this, boy?"

"Yes, Sir, Daddy."

I've never been anybody's daddy, never had a boy to do my bidding. I'm usually the slave, but prefer it rougher than him. I like to be slapped around, called a dirty nigger, fucked by trashy white boys of the South. I'm usually on the other end of the leash. I hawked a thick gob of spit into the crack of his ass. Watched it trundle in. My finger went up in him so easily. I began to wonder how many dicks had gone up that ass before me. All those Georgia balls banging against his booty. I withdrew my finger and moved in a thumb. I tugged at the leash as I finger-fucked him.

"You're my little whore, aren'tcha, boy?" I asked.

"Yes, Sir."

There was no turning back, no running away. The door was locked, the windows were shut, and no one could hear us. His crack was a syrupy mess. My dick was hard and dripping onto the mint-green carpet. Couldn't wait to get my cock in him.

"Turn around," I demanded, pulling at the leash. We switched positions. I held my dick at its base and waved it in his face.

"Suck me, boy." I rolled the slack ends of the chain around my fist. His mouth felt so good on my dick.

"Hard. Deep-throat it."

The tip of his nose tickled as it grazed my musky crotch hair.

"Lick my balls," I said, yanking at the leash. It felt good to be in control for once. I commanded him to stand up. We kissed. I could taste myself on his tongue, on those red lips. He moved down to my nipples and started to suck them. That turned into biting before too long. As teeth sank into my flesh, I pressed his head harder into my chest.

Every nerve ending tingled with pleasure. He bit one nipple, then the other. I felt around. Copped a feel of his ass. All that gluteus flesh in my hands. Slid a finger in again. Good to know that he was still wet with my spit. It was time for the real thing. I had told him in our correspondence that I like to get ridden. I sat on the floor between two La-Z-Boys as he reached for a rubber sitting on a small table next to one of the recliners. My dick was ready for action. He tore the prophylactic out of its red packet. I stared into his face as he rolled the rubber on, covering my dick. He straddled and faced me, sliding my dick up his ass. His insides were so warm. He bucked and rode me into the floor. I knew I would have some fierce carpet burns on my ass to show for it the next morning. You should have heard me. It was like I was speaking in tongues.

"Fuck me, boy," I kept hollering. Best piece of ass I've ever had. I hooked my fingers into the buckles of his boots for leverage, to prevent myself from sliding across the floor. Each time my dick slid out of his butt, he would work it back in.

"Want to fuck me some other way, Daddy?"

I was wondering how long he would be able to stand it. He positioned himself on all fours. Ass was round and white as if he had been drained of blood. I kneeled at it, pressed my hand at the small of his back, at the base of his spine. Pulled at him like the pup he was.

"Lower," I said.

"Yes, Daddy."

"Daddy wants to fuck," I said.

I spat on my dick and massaged it into the latex. I don't care for it doggie-style. My legs are too quick to give out. Gotta get my ass into shape. I got my hard-on in after two fussy attempts. Steady and strong I fucked him. I looked to the window and daydreamed of a voyeuristic neighbor. Or the mailman wandering over, gawking through the plate glass at our actions, rubbing his dick through those polyester shorts they wear during the summer months. My sex swerved in and out of him. The backs of my legs were starting to get the best of me, but I didn't care. He was that good, my perfect, obedient boy-pup.

I warned him that I was about to come.

"Come in me, Daddy," he said. With each thrust, I was getting closer to climaxing. I sank my fingernails into his soft, pale butt and shot white fire up inside him. I pulled out slow and collapsed on top of him.

"Is Daddy pleased?" he asked.

We tumbled over on the floor and faced each other. I took his tongue into my mouth and kissed him hard again. Sloppy and wet. I reached down and squeezed his dick in my palm, the same dick he sent me a photo of in an email attachment.

"Spank me, Daddy."

I gave him a swift slap across his ass.

"Harder, Daddy." I licked both palms and gave him another whack on his behind. Those cheeks of his shaded a pretty rose red in no time. My dick was growing hard again. He broke out of the daze of his submissiveness and said, "I'll be back."

I wondered why he kept dismissing himself. All I could hear from the living room was a toilet being flushed. I grabbed my shirt and began to wipe my face free of perspiration. I could hear the metal of the buckles beat against the tough, black hide of his boots as he made his way back to my naked, corpulent bod. He reappeared with another one of his toys. It was one of those whips with leather tails. I looked up into his pale-blue eyes. He assumed the position awaiting his punishment. I gripped the handle and laid into him. WHAP! He winced as the tails licked his naughty ass. This was all so new to me. I'm used to being on the slave end of the lash.

"Do it harder, Daddy," he said.

I yanked at his collar, forcing his back to arch to my domination as I took it out on his flesh. My dick seeped precum without ever being touched. I caught the string of cum with my finger and flicked it onto his back. After every lash across his ass, he pleaded for more, begged for it to be harder each time.

"Are you a whore?" I asked.

"Daddy's dirty whore," he said.

His dick dangled long between his legs. I tugged at the leash and said, "Up. Get up on the chair." I sat on one end of the sofa while he was splayed out with his legs apart and his pink, cut dick begging for attention. As I slid my hands under his butt, he winced to my touch. His dick was just as immaculate as his ass. He plunged it into my mouth.

"Like this, Daddy?"

I reached up and pulled at the harness. I cradled him into my arms, lifting him into me. His dick tensed; I pinched his nipples hard, his hands bit into the cushion of the couch as I brought the evening to a climactic close. Took it all as he came. I spat him out into that jelly-jar glass of watered-down Gatorade. His face had gone from being deathly white to almost beet red. After we managed to regain our composure, I asked the time, which felt like the wrong thing to ask about.

"Almost eight," he said.

"Daddy's got to get going."

"Is Daddy pleased?" he asked as he kissed me.

"Pleased. Pleased indeed."

Seemed like it took me forever and a day to leave. We kissed one last time at my car. We made another date for that Saturday. He explained that he had to call his girlfriend, that he would be playing the role of the dominant for her sake. He bent between me and my car door. I fingered his asshole for the last time that evening.

"Can't wait until Saturday, boy," I told him. I drove home with his Southern Gothic scent on my skin, his ass and cum lingering on my tongue.

INTRODUCTION

Dan Cullinane

In the right hands, something as innocuously everyday as Velcro can send the doors to your imagination crashing off the hinges. And while we're on the subject of everyday surprises, I'd like to point out that it's entirely possible that your neighbor is making coleslaw in nothing but a studded collar and a pair of knee-high boots.

Learning the truth—the kind of truth that burrows inside and devours you—can be a walk through scouring flames. But sometimes all you can bring yourself to do is to look into the fire.

Master Damon and his lover Wilder wanted to invite a man into their household, a man to train as a slave, a man who would vacuum and take a fist up his ass, who would wash the windows and drink piss. It was kind of complicated.

Go ahead. Laugh. Ignorance is funny when you are on the other side. I get it. But I can't get my head into a place where people are something other than people. Folks are folks, you know? What makes it all remarkable is its relationship to the ordinary. Day-to-day living in unusual circumstances. *Lifestyle* seems such a banal word for it.

As an amateur student of anthropology—which is nothing more than a souped-up way to say "people watcher"—I find this shit fascinating. As long as it's happening to someone other than me. But sometimes the close view singes.

The second time I met Master Damon, he wouldn't talk to me until I was kneeling shirtless on the floor. Because he knew I knew better.

I have this friend, Lady Katherine, who lives in New York. She's a mistress. Not *someone's* mistress; she belongs to no one. Guys belong to her. She has submissives, and she has slaves. Lady Katherine and I have lots of conversations about BDSM, even though I've never walked that path. But I love that she has, and I love her stories, and she's a whip-smart lady who knows I could go there; she kids me about it all the time. I squirm, she laughs. It's been this way for years. One time she took me to a flogging demonstration at some club around Midtown and dared me to get my ass beat. I did, of course, and she laughed so hard she almost fell off her chair. I liked showing my butt to a room full of strangers, and I liked the way the woman's hand felt when she rubbed me, and I liked the heat that radiated through me when she struck me, and I wasn't terribly surprised by any of it. It was just playacting. I laughed, and went home and lay in my bed feeling the slow burn of the welts on my backside, and I laughed some more. Funny as hell, but safer than "Romper Room."

Lady Katherine is very, very good at what she does, and because of that, she also has a submissive in San Diego, where she travels on business. In between sessions where she makes this dude dress up in panties, she makes time for lunch with me, and it's not that far from L.A. to San Diego, so I always drive down. This time, she had errands.

"I need to drop by Damon and Wilder's to pick up a vest," she said over salad.

She never explains who anyone is. She just talks about them like I know them. Or at least like I should. For some reason, I never ask, either.

"I need you to drive me," she finished.

"Okay."

"You'll like their shop," she said, offering no further information. I didn't ask.

She was right, of course. Their shop is a kick-ass place. It's a converted garage at the end of their driveway, walls lined with leather hoods and harnesses and restraints. Stacks of photo albums showcase their gear. They do amazing custom work, making leather pants, vests, wristbands, coats, whatever anyone wants. They have rock star clients. Like, real rock stars. It's like Folsom Street meets Rodeo Drive.

Damon moved around the shop like a prize-fighter. Handsome in a dark Irish way that made you look three times before you asked yourself why you kept looking at this guy, his eyes twinkled like rhinestones one minute and turned to flint the next. Good businessman that he is, he gave me a tour of the shop. I didn't know what I was looking at really, but I didn't want to be a dork, so I pretended it was all totally familiar.

Lady Katherine watched me, a small smile cutting across her face as I tripped over my ignorance.

"He's not in the scene, Damon," she said finally.

Damon faked surprise. "Oh, I couldn't tell. You seemed so sure of yourself."

Lady Katherine laughed happily.

"So do you want to try anything on?" he continued.

"Yes. Yes you do." Lady Katherine chimed in merrily.

This was the moment, a friend later told me, when I no doubt twitched my tail like a little bunny rabbit. Which is insulting. Also true.

From cocky to passive-aggressive in three point five seconds, I responded by saying, "I don't really know anything. I wouldn't even know what to try." Twitch.

Some part of Damon was in constant motion and yet he was tranquil, in a storm-reflected-on-the-surface-of-a-pond sort of way. He was infuriatingly unflappable.

"You don't know anything? And yet you drove over here. That's really scary. Good thing you got someone to tie your shoes for you." I later learned that sometimes it amuses him to take your words and toss them all over the place like a big kid holding your toy out of reach. "Well, if you knew something, do you think you might like this?"

He led me by the arm to the other side of the shop, his grip insistent, like a cop pushing you into the backseat of his cruiser. He yanked a simple harness off the wall and handed it to me.

"Take your shirt off."

I looked at him. There was nothing on his face other than the look of a salesman trying to make a sale. I swallowed, and slipped my shirt over my head. He strapped the harness around my chest, then took my shoulders and propelled me in front of the mirror.

There I was, my skinny, pale chest encased in straps and buckles that hung off me unflatteringly. A Titan video I wasn't. It was agonizing to see. I attempted to overcome my discomfort by scoffing.

"Yeah, well, so. I mean it's nice, but what is it supposed to do?"

I had turned from the mirror, and Damon was now standing directly in front of me. It wasn't as if his eyes actually had changed color, but I could have sworn they were suddenly darker: I can't explain this. They were definitely harder. The chatty salesman had taken a coffee break and turned me over to the guy who flips the switch on the electric chair.

His voice hadn't gotten deeper or louder or anything stupidly obvious like that. In fact it was, if anything, softer. And every word was clipped and excruciatingly enunciated. "What. Is. Its. Purpose?" he asked, as though I were a stunningly slow first-grader.

I felt like a worm.

His right hand shot out, grabbed the metal ring centered on my chest, and yanked me toward him so hard my feet left the ground. He pulled me tight against his body, his eyes never leaving mine, then swung me around, threw me down over the workbench, and slammed his hips into me.

"Well, I can do that with it," he said, his voice little more than a hot breath against my ear.

"Let's go outside," I heard Lady Katherine say softly, and from my position, facedown over the workbench, I saw her and Wilder's silhouettes against the open door for a moment, and then they were gone. I had stopped breathing when Damon slammed into me, and now I let it go, trying not to whimper.

Damon released me, and I turned around.

"Well," I said with a nervous laugh, "I think I get that one now."

I caught my breath, startled but also thrilled.

I might have been ready to find out what else you could do in a workshop on a sunny Sunday afternoon while wearing a leather harness. But the salesman had returned, and there I was all dressed up, with no one to notice. That icky squirmy feeling returned, and I avoided looking in the mirror.

Like a frontier peddler, Damon began rapidly showing me more, pulling wrist restraints off the wall and explaining how beefalo hide is softer and doesn't wear. I learned that their restraints don't cause chafing even after repeated use, and that their prices are lower than their competitors. He had the price lists to prove it, and showed them to me.

I joined in, pretending like mad that my interest was purely commercial, nodding and asking questions about bulk pricing and exclusive designs. I knew someone who had a website, did he offer commercial discounts? Yes indeed, special pricing could be arranged, and as far as exclusive designs, well.... Damon whirled around to show me an original design for wrist-to-thigh restraints.

"Give me your hand," he said.

I did. This time I didn't even bother to pretend that this was research.

He buckled my wrist into the strap, and then cinched the belt around my waist, leaving one hand free.

"Now your other hand." His eyes locked on me, shifting again. He took my wrist before I could offer it, and strapped both wrists to the belt around my waist.

We faced each other.

"I can do anything I want to you now."

Quietly the salesman had again left the room. This time it didn't surprise me. I had been expecting it. I had been hoping for it. I welcomed it. I didn't know exactly what it meant, but I hoped to before the afternoon was over.

"I could get you on your knees right now. If. I. Wanted. To," Damon informed me, calmly and clearly.

My mouth was too dry to speak, not that I could think of anything to say, anyway.

I just stared directly into his hard dark eyes and willed myself not to blink. Somehow I thought that if I didn't look away, if I didn't drop my eyes, I was not giving myself over to this. Which was weird because I wanted to. I just couldn't. Which might have been weirder.

"I could do things to you that would make your toes curl. You. Know. That."

"I'm sure you could," I said with a deeply fought-for, casual sounding laugh. "I'm sure you could."

And then he changed again. But not back into the salesman. He was still pushing me, but it became playful.

"Are you ticklish?" he asked.

I am. Horribly. Uncontrollably. I've been known to vomit.

He ran his hands up my sides into my armpits and began tickling me, sending me into convulsions, and a backward stumbling retreat around the table. The moment shattered, blown away by giggling. He released me from the restraints.

"What about cock rings?" he asked.

"I've never worn one." I'm embarrassed to say that at that point in my life, that was a true statement. He was as surprised about it then as I am now.

"You're kidding. You've never worn a cock ring? Well, try it out."

"Sorry, I'm kind of a prude." This said shirtless, while wearing a leather harness. But I think I meant it.

"Okay. That's fine." From a beam over his head, he whipped off a mystifying jumble of leather and metal. "This is another exclusive design. It's called a riding saddle."

It was a wide leather belt with multiple straps, and two large metal rings hanging off of it. On the kind of saddles I am familiar with, loops are generally stirrups, and I found that stimulating.

"How does that work?" I asked.

But Damon was bored now, sick of my wide-eyed routine.

"Oh, okay, well, turn around," he said, but his voice had no edge, his hands were perfunctory.

He slipped the wide belt around my waist and used the narrow belts to tighten it. Then, with his hands in the loops, he pulled me tightly against him again, his crotch against my butt.

"Like that. Now turn around and sit down."

I sat in the studded leather chair he'd indicated, and he grabbed my legs and looped them over his elbows, thrust his hands into the loops and pulled me against him once more.

"And like that."

But it wasn't there this time. This was just about fucking, and I've been fucked. Damon's heart wasn't in it anymore, and I was starting to feel like I was playing dress-up.

I knew there was more he could show me, and I wanted more, and he knew that. But here's the deal. You have to be willing. You have to show up for this stuff. I was trying to push him into taking me by force. But a power exchange doesn't occur when power is taken. It has to be given away. I didn't know that, though.

There were a few steps I needed to take. Very few, in fact. I didn't count them as I followed him into his bedroom, but there couldn't have been more than twenty-five. Here's how that happened:

Damon helped me out of the saddle and the harness, and I pulled my safe little gray T-shirt back over my head.

Lady Katherine and Wilder wandered back in, looking thoroughly innocent and not at all curious about what might have taken place in their absence.

I mostly had my composure back, and Damon had jumped right back into business-as-usual.

"In addition," he said, "we personally try out all of our products before we sell them. Anything you see here has been tested by us before we put it in the catalog."

"Did you see their bedroom?" Lady Katherine asked

Wondering how she thought that might have been possible—or why—I lobbed a filthy look her way.

"No. No, I didn't."

"Oh, you should," she positively chirped, all wide-eyed innocence. "They have a wonderful setup. Oh, and Damon, Wilder showed me the stained glass. It's beautiful."

"Do you want to see it?" Damon asked me.

And they all just stood there looking at me. The three of them, completely aware of what was happening, watching me carefully, without expression, to see what my next move would be.

And of course that's why I said yes, because no way was I backing down.

Their house always leaves me a little at a loss for words. I've been there a few times now, though, so the impact has lessened.

"I have a thing for Nikolay Alexandrovich Romanov," Damon told me as we walked out of the shop and into his home. "He was the last sitting czar of Russia at the time of the revolution."

Which explained one collection.

"Wilder made all the ships," he continued.

Which explained another collection.

The skulls, phalluses, and other artifacts were not explained as we passed through the room on the way to the bedroom. Really, they don't need explanation. They are just there, mixed in with all the rest in a sort of fantastic museum of dark depravity. It works, really it does. But it's not a large place. So on first glance, it takes some adjustment.

I followed Damon down a short hallway, so completely, obliviously turned on I was practically humping his leg. The bedroom was like a bucket of cold water.

I glancingly noticed the stained glass piece that took up most of the one small window. The leather flag, very nice. I also noticed that the walls were painted deep red, which I always think is a very bold color choice for a small space.

My eyes were riveted on the bed. Actually it's hard to say

where the bed began. There was a bed there, an apple-green comforter hastily drawn up and a red satin heart-shaped pillow embroidered with I LOVE YOU tossed against the headboard. But it crouched like an afterthought below a black wooden structure studded with pegs and hooks, and wrapped with ropes and straps. From the ceiling a spiderweb canopy of silver chains reached down menacingly, like a canopy bed from *Hellraiser*.

"This is where we try everything out," Damon told me. "Those restraints I was showing you, they're right here," he said, indicating the top of the entertainment center. The bedside table was littered with cock rings, the way some people's might be littered with loose change.

He unlooped a rope from what I decided was a bedpost, and a bar with metal loops at either end dropped from the top of the canopy. This is called a spreader. It needs no explanation, and I didn't ask for one.

"Try this," he said, uncuffing a restraint from the bedpost. "You think of Velcro, you think pretty harmless right? Put your wrist in here."

This demonstration was the one that counted, and I knew it, and I did it anyway.

"Now put your hand in the other one." He secured both restraints to the ends of the spreader, and pulled the rope tight, looping it around a nail. There I was, spread. Basically hanging and willingly helpless.

"Velcro. Can you believe it? Try to get loose."

I gamely made a few halfhearted attempts to loosen the restraints, knowing it was pointless, and then gave up.

His hands slid under my shirt, not really tickling, not really stroking, just moving lightly over my skin, like a misgiving.

"I can tickle you again now," he said.

I squirmed against the restraints. His hands were in my armpits, insistent and intrusive.

"You can't move, can you?" he asked.

"No, I can't."

"You. Like. This. Don't. You?"

And suddenly I didn't. In this short moment, something inside me began to scream, and kept on screaming.

Maybe it was the darkness of the room, maybe it was that change in his voice and his eyes again, but this was different from what happened in the shop. He was more serious now, and I realized very quickly that my stupid little game was about to get real. And what was scarier still, I didn't know what that meant.

I groped around with my foot until I found the headboard, and then I was standing on the edge of the bed, trying to escape.

"Careful," he said, drawing his hands away. "You'll hit your head on the ceiling fan."

I felt safer now—still restrained, but safer—and, laughing a little, I stepped off the bed frame.

"How do you feel?" he asked.

I had wanted it to stop. Now I wanted it to start again. Without his hands I felt bereft.

"I don't know. Weird. This is weird. I've never done anything like this before."

"But...and correct me if I'm wrong...I think you have fantasized about this. A lot."

I looked away, at the door, at the daylight pouring into the hallway just beyond it.

"Yeah, I suppose. Yes."

"And what's scary is letting yourself live your own fantasy."

"I don't know. I don't know why it's scary. I mean, everyone fantasizes about this stuff sometimes."

"Yes. They do."

He pulled me toward him, his hand cupping my neck, and pulled my forehead against his chest while he whispered in my ear.

"There is nothing scary about any of this. What's scary is letting yourself actually go to places that you have so far only visited safely, in your imagination."

I was still spread-eagle, and his hands began roaming again, up under my shirt.

"In your fantasies, you can let yourself be darker than you want to believe you can actually be. What's frightening is finding out that you might be darker, in fact, than your own fantasies."

His hands moved down, unzipped my shorts, and slid inside.

"Hmm," he breathed in my ear. "What's this? What do we have here?"

I was trembling, and felt almost liquid. But I wasn't hard. I couldn't have gotten hard if my life had depended on it.

"You can't do anything about this." He told me as if I didn't already know it.

"I know." It came out as a whisper. "I know. But please don't do it."

His hand stopped moving, then drew away. He zipped my shorts.

"Okay." His normal voice had returned. "I thought you wanted to go a little further."

"I did. I do. But I can't."

He unfastened my arms and pulled me against him again. I was shaking so hard, I know that he felt it, but his chest was warm and big and safe, and I didn't care. His arms around me felt secure, and as he rocked me against him, I felt my face collapse and I started to cry. My hands were hanging limply at my sides, my whole weight leaning against him, and he just held me while I shook and cried.

"This is what I do," he said softly. "I test the limits. Everyone is different. You are just beginning to explore yours. This is as far as it goes. For now."

I wanted this so bad. I didn't know why I was fighting it. I didn't know what surrendering to it meant, but that screaming inside me wouldn't let me do it. I felt like I was so close to something. Something I wanted, but something that would devour me, so nothing would be left. I wanted what was on the other side, but I couldn't give in. I couldn't give myself away, and I grieved for what remained out of reach, for what I wouldn't find, and for the small part of me that changed forever by realizing it.

"You know how sometimes you walk down a dark alley," he continued, "and you know you shouldn't do it, but you do anyway? You know why you do that? Because of the feeling you get on the other side when you make it through safely."

He pushed me back from him, and I swiped at my eyes. I felt very small. We began to move toward the door, toward the sunlight.

"Wait," he said, pulling a cap off the dresser. "You should see what I look like when I go out."

It was either a military cap or a motorcycle cap, or a combination of both, decorated with an insignia I didn't recognize. He pulled it down low over his brow, and strapped on a couple of leather wristbands, and then glowered at me.

"Pretty scary, huh?" he asked.

"Sure. Very."

He put his hands on my shoulders and pushed me back onto the bed, standing over me. I was unrestrained but still immobile, and scared again.

He pulled me toward him, and I felt the cool leather of his wristbands against my cheek.

"This," he whispered in my ear, "that you feel against your cheek, this is beefalo. What the fuck is beefalo? And this cap? This cap is Harley Davidson. Harley Davidson. I don't even own a motorbike. How stupid is that? And Velcro. Before, just now, when you were strapped up there, that was Velcro. How scary is Velcro?"

I was shaking again. My forehead was pressed tightly against his chest as he stroked my cheek, his breath hot against my ear. I felt more trapped, more unable to move than when he had me strapped up.

"There is nothing scary here. The only thing that's scary is your imagination. You create everything here. It's all you."

He lifted my head, a warm hand under my chin.

"This bed? We painted it black. We could have painted it chartreuse; it wouldn't have made any difference. All of this, all it does, is unlock your own fantasies. It's only as scary as you want it to be."

I nodded, hating myself because I had started crying again.

"I want to ask you something, and then we can go back outside. Back into the sunshine."

"Okay."

"Can I kiss you?"

"What if I say no?"

"Then we go back outside, and I don't get a kiss."

"Oh."

"Just a little kiss." His finger touched a spot on the edge of my mouth. "Right there."

I felt myself smiling. I wanted this kiss.

"I'm going to kiss you right there." His finger was still on the spot as he leaned into me. "Right there," and then his finger was replaced by his lips. I kept my mouth shut for just a second, and then kissed him back, only a little. His tongue ran against my lips, but his mouth never moved from that one spot. It lasted for a good thirty seconds, his hand hard against the back of my head, but just in that one spot on my upper lip, never moving to claim my whole mouth.

Then it was over, his voice returned to normal, and we walked outside.

This I know. My tongue never even touched the ice cream. I didn't even smell the sugar. I know that.

But I spent an hour with a master and began to understand the power that goes with that title. Am I susceptible? Of course I am. If I wasn't, it wouldn't have happened, but I'm also a skeptic about titles and role-playing.

Damon met me, saw something, and got inside my head in a few short minutes. Granted, I showed my hand early on, but during that little scene in the bedroom, he knew exactly what to say, what to push, how hard, and when to pull back. He knew holding me that way would calm me enough, and that kissing me would make everything okay.

And that's what pulled me in. Because if he could do that to me in that short amount of time, what could he do with a slave?

After we went outside, Damon and I sat in the backyard, just the two of us. He told me he was looking for a slave to train. He told me that he had been trained as a slave, years before, by a woman. He told me he had once, on orders, nailed his testicles to a piece of wood. I changed my mind about offering to be his slave.

After we left, Lady Katherine and I went for Thai food. I ate my green curry mostly in silence. If she was curious about what had happened she didn't show it. It was more than a year before I told her. She told me that she knew she could trust Damon, and that she would never have let me walk away with him if that wasn't the case.

It was dark when I hit the 5 headed back to L.A. Lights flashed past. I was buzzing. The development of a slave. What did that mean? What would it take? I was in Oceanside before the cold fear inside me began to warm. I knew then that I was less interested in the physical aspect of it. Floggings, restraints, humiliation, pain, whatever—to me those were just trappings. What was it Damon said? "You create everything here. It's all you."

Damon and Wilder found a slave, and because that journey was something I wanted to know more about, but didn't want to take myself, I watched from a distance. I recorded it, and I wrote the story of it. I had returned to the house, and asked for permission, shirtless and on my knees because that was the appropriate thing to do. I watched their household and I wrote and wrote about what I saw and heard, looking for iconic figures and finding only people. The people living next door, day to day, in the most unusual of circumstances. It's what you bring to it.

And yeah, I've pushed myself further on occasion, taking another bite in another city with another man. I might do it again. I might not. Because it's up to me, and I'm not sure I have it in me. I always imagined it was something I could do against my will, almost—as an observer rather than a participant. I've wished it was something that could be forced upon me, something that could be taken. But it's something that must be given, and that still frightens me, holds me at the end of the leash, tugging ever so slightly, but never hard enough to break the tether. I guess I'm still looking for the icon. The man who can own me, without my agreeing to be owned.

COMMUNITY PUNISHMENT: THE STORY OF A BRITISH RENT PIG

Thom Wolf

I knew Callum from my work with the Probation Service, when he was just another pretty-faced waster under my supervision. He was on probation for stealing a car and driving under the influence of alcohol. The police found him seventy miles from home, lucky to be alive, after smashing into a wall. He was a sixteen-year-old fuck-up, one of the first cases allocated to me in the Young Offenders Department.

He was a hopeless cause, always late for his appointments, often drunk and abusive. He took no responsibility for his actions, minimizing the damage he had done and learning nothing. He was untidy, antisocial, and aggressive. A no-hope pain in the arse, but a pain in the arse I was happy to endure.

Callum was the kind of boy who could get a certain kind of older man into trouble. I wasn't one of them, not then—my career was too important—but I have never wanted to fuck another one of my surly teen delinquents the way I wanted to fuck that boy.

Beneath the dour expressions, the messy haircut, and the baggy, often unwashed clothes, there was an astonishingly beautiful kid. His mother was white trash but the coloring of the boy's skin—dark, even in winter—and his jet black hair suggested Southern European blood, maybe gypsy, on his father's side.

He was gorgeous and he knew it. When I was around him I was always hard, always turned on. He knew what to do, how best to play with me: twisting me round his finger, promising to stay straight when his eyes were so clouded with drink and drugs that he couldn't even look straight. He would lean closer in the interview room—so close I could feel the warmth of his breath, smell the alcohol fumes against my face—and beg me not to send him back to court, to keep him out of the young offenders institution. So beautiful, so tender, so conniving.

Despite the work I did with him, all the effort I made to enforce his punishment in the community, he couldn't keep out of trouble. There was one time when he turned up for an appointment in a leather jacket; it was black, biker style. It suited him, an ideal choice for such a bad boy. It was new and smelled really good. I asked him where he nicked it from. He just laughed and changed the subject, though he wore the jacket to every appointment after that.

He drank heavily, and in drink he got nasty, violent. When he ceased attending his appointments, I had no choice but to enforce the order and summon him back to court. A court date was set, but when the day arrived he failed to attend and a warrant was issued for his arrest. Callum went on the run and the police never caught up with him.

Eventually his file was removed from my caseload and placed in the warrants drawers and that was the end of my official involvement with beautiful, fucked-up little Callum.

Three years later, looking through the back pages of a gay

monthly, where the rent boys and escorts advertise their services, I saw his face again, looking older, longer in the jaw, harder round the eyes, but I had no doubt—it was him. I'd recognize the bastard anywhere.

The ad and the photograph were small, just a thumbnail picture and a few lines of text: *North East. No attitude bottom boy 19. Out calls only.* A mobile number was listed along with the web address for his Gaydar profile. The photo showed his face and shoulders, unsmiling, seemingly naked. His dark hair was buzz cut, which accentuated the hard expression on his face; the lines that were etched there told me all I needed to know about his life since he disappeared.

Callum, what have you been up to? I thought.

I dialed the number. The voice that answered, with a businesslike "Hello," sent an old, familiar jolt to my cock. Any vestige of doubt was gone; one word, monotone and flat, told me I had found my boy.

The call was short and to the point. He asked me what I wanted and talked up his services as a bottom extraordinaire, before quoting me a basic rate per hour. Listening to his dirty talk made my cock ache harder. I wanted to shove my dick down his throat, muffling the ballsy chat. Choking the attitude. I wanted to pound his no-good arse and fuck him for every bit of arrogance he, and boys of his type, had ever shown me in my work.

We made a deal and I gave him directions to my house. If my mind had been working more wisely than my dick, I might have thought twice about inviting a proven thief, drunk, and whore to my home, but realizing a three-year-old fantasy was more vital than safety. If he recognized me, if he remembered who I was, he could ruin me. I was opening myself to blackmail but that didn't matter; riding his bad-boy arse did.

He arrived half an hour late, making no apology for his lateness, and stood on the street, one hand moving down the front of his pants while I paid his taxi fare. I glanced quickly round the neighboring houses. Just a couple of lights were showing behind closed blinds. There was not much sign of life in the suburbs at 3:30 A.M.

I turned to look at Callum, who was already watching me. His face was unsmiling and unemotional. "Just so you know," he said. "The driver is a friend of mine. If I don't make it home he'll remember where he left me." His words were fractured with unusual pauses, like a drunkard in a pub, trying to make a point.

"That's wise of you but you don't have to worry about me," I said. "I'm only paying you for the two hours we agreed."

He nodded, almost smiling, not quite.

"Let's go in," I told him. "I want to see you better."

With his hand still fumbling in his pants, he made a move toward the house, heading for the front door. I told him "No," and led him to the garage. My car was parked in the driveway, leaving plenty of space inside. I pulled a cord, turning on a naked lightbulb that illuminated dusty concrete floors, rows of shelving, old paint tins, a lawn mower, furniture in storage, and a small refrigerator.

The harsh light bleached the olive skin of Callum's face. He narrowed his eyes against the glare. He was wearing baggy jeans and the leather jacket I remembered, worn and rough now, over a washed-out rock T-shirt. For an escort he was down at the lower end of the scale. He took off the jacket and I was pleased to see that his skinny arms were free of track marks or obvious scarring.

"Have you got any booze?" he asked. "My mouth is bone dry."

I told him to take off his shirt while I got him a beer. I watched him as I moved to the fridge. He pulled the T-shirt over his head, revealing a torso that was thin, but not as scrawny as I'd imagined it to be. He would benefit from a few more meals and a little less drink, but he was in much better shape than I expected.

He swayed slightly while waiting for the beer. I wanted him to look at me, to look full into my face, so I'd see if he recognized me, but he was entirely disinterested. I knew all he really wanted was my booze and my money, but it still bothered me that he couldn't fake a small amount of interest for the man about to bust his arse.

I hitched my butt onto the lid of the fridge and told him to take everything off. He drained a can of beer, spilling golden, foamy liquid over his chest and rounded belly, before shaking off his jeans. He hopped around on one foot, then the other, drawing the jeans into an inside-out tangle before tossing them away onto the bare and dusty floor. Something thudded heavily against the concrete, a weight in the pocket of his jeans. Gun? Knife? Nothing would surprise me.

I could handle it if I had to.

His legs were long and hairy while his cock was long and soft—as much as I'd expect from a drunk. He stood in front of me, tugging his dick into a semistiff state, completely unembarrassed by his nakedness. That sight alone could have made me come. "Put your jacket back on," I said. "Just the jacket."

He scowled but did as he was told, pulling the black leather jacket back over his arms. He pulled the zipper up to the neck. The sight of him in that leather, his lower body naked, was visual dynamite. There may even have been a slight swelling of his cock.

Next I told him to turn around and show me his arse, which

was round and juicy. His buttcheeks were covered in a tasty brown fur, which followed the curve toward his middle, growing thicker and darker in the crack. He leaned forward when I told him to, shoving back his hips and opening himself up with both hands.

Nice, I thought, as his arsehole was pulled into a gape. In time with the beat of my heart, his anus pulsed open and closed.

Possessed by greed, I left my vantage point. I pushed him over, his hands to his ankles, arse stuck high, and worked his butt with my hands, spanking his arsecheeks till their color changed from cream to pink to a stinging shade of red. I spat gobs of saliva over his buttocks, smacking my spit into his skin. He flinched a little, gasped a bit, but took the beating like a man. The sound of hand against skin echoed like gunfire against the bare walls.

Nasty fingers got stuck into his spit-lubed ring—straight in with two, working quickly to five. I shoved in and out of his professional hole, right in to the knuckle. I wondered, as I fingerfucked him, how many men had made use of this opening since he started work that day? How many hands, cocks, and tongues had entered his back door?

He breathed heavily, growling low, never complaining. The Callum I knew of old bitched and whined about everything. He'd taken it all for granted; nothing was ever good enough. A hand up the arse was good enough for the bastard now.

I ordered him to lie on his back across the fridge, knees into his chest and arsehole open wide. His brown eyes stared at me as I fingered his juicy snatch. There was a glimmer of recognition, just a hint. He recognized my face, but did he know where from?

He lay there waiting while I undressed. I took off everything before putting back on my thick-soled leather boots. The leather is tan colored and scuffed, grimy from the dust, lube, and spunk of god knows how many dark rooms and toilets. They were my favorite boots. I still wore a black leather cock strap that I'd fitted 'round the base of my balls and dick before Callum arrived. The fit was nice and tight, holding my nuts and hard cock in a forward position.

Callum was unfazed when I stuck a dildo into his big brown hole. There was minimal resistance from his sphincter, and I buried nine inches of fat black rubber into him with barely any effort. His passivity amazed me, but it also began to annoy me. I spat right into his face, hoping for a reaction; he closed his eyes for only a moment before licking his lips and opening his mouth, so that my next deposit landed straight on his tongue.

I drew the dildo back and forth and twisted its length inside him. If Callum was fazed by the huge intrusion in his arse, it didn't show on his face. All the while his erection was little more than semihard.

When I'd churned his arse into a sloppy pink gash, I was ready to fuck him. I put on a condom and shoved right in, hooking his knees around my elbows for maximum leverage. It was difficult, as I fucked him, not to think about his past—his troubled childhood, the crime-riddled teen years, alcohol, drugs—but I felt nothing in the way of sympathy. Fucking his arse for my own pleasure was his punishment. This was community service, retribution and rehabilitation rolled into one.

I fucked him hard and rough, for every kid he had intimidated, every car he'd stolen, every purse he'd snatched. I fucked him for the fear he'd caused, the inconvenience and heartbreak. I fucked because it was all I'd ever wanted to do to him.

I pulled out when ready, ripping off the rubber to spray my load into his wide-open mouth. His eyes stared helplessly as the bitter milk poured over his tongue, filling his mouth.

"Eat it," I ordered. "Eat every drop."

Callum closed his mouth and swallowed, grimacing slightly, fighting the urge to gag. I brought my cock closer to his sealed lips, smearing cum across the surface. He opened again and sucked me, slurping my dick till it was clean.

While he put on his clothes, I counted out the money onto the surface of the fridge.

"Can I have another beer before I go? I've got to get rid of this taste."

The boy I used to know would not have asked; he'd have taken.

"No," I told him. "You take the taste of me with you. Now get out."

"I know who you are," he said. "Trent."

"When did you realize?"

"Week or so; knew I'd seen your face before, just wasn't sure where. Thought you might have been a client. Knew you weren't, of course. I always remember the bastards." He didn't smile. "Should I be worried?"

I allowed the question to hang in the air for a long time before answering. "I haven't decided yet. Go now if you want."

"No. You're paying, I'll stay."

It was seven weeks after the night in my garage. This time I took him in the house, though we went straight up the stairs to the bedroom, where there was little of value for him to steal.

The curtains were drawn against the weak November sun. The lights were on and in the corner of the room a video camera was mounted on a tripod, pointing toward the bed. "I want to film us this time."

Callum's eyes moved between my face and the camera, then back to me. "All right," he said, agreeing on a price for this extra.

His behavior was different than before. He was sober, for a start. He seemed unsure of himself, quiet. I wondered again what had happened to him in the last three years to bring about such a change of character; he bore nothing but a physical resemblance to the cocky offender who was once under my supervision. What kind of hardships had forced him from a life of petty crime into prostitution?

I can't pretend I really cared. I could have helped him in the past if he had wanted me to, when it was still my job to help him. I was paid to lend a hand back then; now I was paying him to give up his arse. It was a situation massively improved.

Turning on the camera, I ordered him to strip. He did as he was told, always looking downward, never at me or my camera. His body was bruised around the stomach and thighs and there were scratches on his arms. A rough client, I wondered, or a fight with another hustler? I didn't ask. I gave him a leather dog collar to wear, black and studded. He looked unsure but put it on like I told him.

I was already dressed: a black leather waistcoat that fastened up to just below my chest, showing off my hairy tits, and heavy black boots that came all the way to my knees. A leather strap was fixed firmly around my cock and balls. I lit a cigar, a fat Don Julian, and inhaled the smoke as I watched him, getting a high from the fumes.

"Spread your arse," I directed. "Open up so I can see it." I trained the camera on his gaping buttcheeks, closing in on the pouting arsehole. His sphincter tightened, pulsing like a tiny mouth, showing hints of dusky pink interior when open. The spectacle had a profound effect upon my cock. The last time he had been here I wanted to play with his ring, to explore it and test its limits. This time I just wanted to fuck it.

Callum moved exactly how I wanted him to, bending over

the bed, spreading his legs, hips pushed back for the inevitable. I loosened his arsehole with a few grasping fingers, pushing and probing. I took another deep breath from the cigar before exhaling the smoke onto his arsehole. Feathery tendrils of smoke danced across his ring and seemed to cling to the sweaty creases. I kissed his arse, tasting the profusion of boy and cigar.

I shoved lube deep into his hole. What little resistance remaining in his sphincter soon disappeared. It was a loose, juicy opening now, ripe for penetration.

When I pulled my fingers out of his arse and offered them to his mouth, Callum opened up and sucked them clean with no hesitation.

You dumb, horny, desperate fool, I thought as I fed him the juices of his rectum on my fingers. That single act was enough to convince me that this was a boy who would do absolutely anything to survive. He probably had, hundreds of times before. I could only guess at the depths he had dived to, the degradation he'd accepted, just to get by. The notion thrilled me. I could do anything I wanted to this screwed-up cunt and he'd allow it.

I put on a rubber, for my own sake rather than his, and shoved my cock deep into his arse—all the way with a single lunge. Callum gasped but didn't complain. Holding his hips for leverage I fucked him like a rabid jackrabbit—hard, fast, and merciless, entirely for my own pleasure. The impact of my hips on his butt was a satisfyingly loud and rhythmic crack, which increased in volume as our bodies dripped with sweat. I got a foot up onto the bed and gave it to him harder. I grabbed the leather collar on his neck for leverage and pounded his arse. He cried throughout like a true bottom, seeming to be in pain, but loving every moment of attention. I tightened my hold on the collar, twisting until I heard him choke. His struggle to breathe turned me on. I felt more reckless with him than ever.

It thrilled me to pull out aggressively and watch the momentary gape of his hole before re-plugging the opening with my dick. It takes me a long time to come when I'm fucking. I can hold out for a good thirty to forty minutes, when most men I know can barely last half that time. Like the time before, Callum did not get hard while I fucked him, but neither did he complain or ask me to ease up. It was just as well he didn't; I'm not sure I could have stopped myself.

I smacked his arse with my hand. It wasn't the playful slap of a lover, but the uncontrolled action of a man possessed. I hit him hard, wanting to cause genuine pain. His small round butt reddened beneath my hand. I looked at the old bruises on his body and was determined to match them. I wanted to leave my mark on him, just like his other tricks had done.

When I was ready, I pulled out, ordering him to his knees so I could finish myself off on his face. He didn't close his eyes or even flinch as I sprayed my messy white load onto his face. This time I didn't have to tell him to clean my cock with his mouth. He did it automatically.

"What happened to the arrogant little bastard I used to know?"

Callum sat, half-dressed on the edge of the bed, in just his T-shirt and a single sock, its companion hanging limply in his left hand. He regarded me with the kind of blank expression I didn't understand, but which was a trait of the new rent boy Callum. "He had to grow up."

"Along with the rest of the world. But why? What changed?"

"Fuck off. You're not my probation officer now." He put on the other sock and stood up, looking for his jeans.

"What am I then? A trick? Is that what you would call me?"

"You're a cunt. A sick cocksucker."

I hid my delight. This was more like it; a revelation of the kid I used to know. The kid I always wanted. "*You* sucked *my* cock," I stated firmly. "I haven't even touched yours."

"Give me my fucking money."

"Ask me nicely, Callum."

"I could ruin you if I wanted. It can't be right, what you're doing, even after all this time. You were in a position of trust."

I hit him, hard, right across the face. It was a gut reaction that shocked me almost as much as it did him. "I've no doubt you could ruin me. If there wasn't still a warrant out for your arrest, then maybe you would." I smiled. It felt cold, even to myself. "Your arse may not be worth as much in prison but it'll definitely be popular, don't you think so?"

Callum glowered at me. He patted the pockets of his jeans, searching for something.

"If you're looking for your flick knife, I took it earlier. Those things are dangerous."

His mouth tightened. "Give me what you owe me."

"You'll get it, Callum. You'll get everything you deserve." I put my foot up on the bed and pointed at my grimy boots. "Now get down. We aren't done yet."

THE VILLAGE PERSON

Simon Sheppard

Zack's roommate Carlos broke the news: "Did you hear? One of the Village People will be visiting the ward!"

Carlos had a tone of breathless excitement mixed with wry irony, but it was hard for Zack to care much one way or the other. He was, after all, hooked up to an oxygen machine with a Hickman catheter stuck through his chest. And he had never been much into disco, anyway, except for maybe Sylvester. While everybody, straight people in the burbs especially, had been dancing around to the Village People's "YMCA" and "In the Navy," Zack had been more into the Sex Pistols and the New York Dolls.

"God, Carlos, calm down," Zack croaked—*did he really croak that pathetically?* he marveled. Well, yes he did. "Didn't you see *Can't Stop the Music*?"

"Toots, how could you expect them to make a good movie if the star was Bruce Fucking Jenner?"

Zack sighed through the flood of oxygen.

"Besides," Carlos smiled, "it's the Leatherman...."

But when the Village Person showed up at the AIDS ward, it wasn't *the* Leatherman. Despite the guy's black cowhide outfit, even Zack knew enough about the group to recognize that. "You're not the real deal, are you?" Zack asked him, trying to be as cheeky as Johnny Rotten, if Johnny Rotten had been terminally ill. No, not "terminally," not necessarily, or at least that's what the doctors were trying to convince him. There was this new drug, AZT, in the pipeline, they said, and if he could just hold on until then...

"Guilty as charged," said the Leatherman. "Scott Stein. I replaced Glenn for a while when he wanted to take a break from touring."

"You're handsome, though," Zack gasped. More handsome than the real thing, if his memory served, though his big handlebar mustache wasn't any more to Zack's taste than Glenn Hughes's was.

"Well, thanks," the Leatherman smiled. "You're not bad yourself."

"You're kidding, right?" Zack could just imagine the stunning impression he, semi-emaciated and surrounded by machines, was making. Oh, well. It was flattery, a moment in a charity appearance by a singer who wasn't even a has-been, more a never-was. Or was Zack being crankily ungenerous? Oh well, if anyone had a reason to be a bitch, he did.

"No, I mean it. You may be sick...right now...but it's easy to see you're a babe."

"Underneath the lesions?"

Scott the Leatherman didn't reply. Instead, he laid his hand on Zack's leg.

That felt nice.

And then the leather-clad arm moved, the hand gliding

farther up Zack's leg, up to just inches away from his crotch. Zack nervously glanced over to the next bed. Carlos was totally out of it. Morphine drip. And there was no nurse in sight.

"That feels nice."

The hand moved all the way up to his basket and gave it a squeeze. Despite everything, Zack was getting hard.

"Fuck," he said, "it's been a long time."

"You want me to stop?"

"You kidding?"

Scott the Leatherman gently slid his hand under Zack's blanket and pulled up his flimsy hospital gown. Zack dimly recalled that one of the group—was it the cop?—was straight, but this Leatherman guy clearly knew his way around other men's dicks. His grip was firm but warm, his pace perfect. And, whatever his other talents, he understood what to do with a foreskin.

Zack closed his eyes. Everything—the oxygen feed, the tube in his chest, the drip, the smell of the room, his illness—it all went away, drained out of him by the pleasure he was feeling.

It would have been unrealistic to claim that Zack could actually *feel* that the hand was worshipping his cock, rather than just jacking it off. But that's what it seemed like. And he wasn't going to argue.

"How's that feel, buddy?"

Zack wished that the Village Person hadn't snapped him out of his erotic trance. He was back in the hospital, on the edge, maybe, of death...but *even so* what was happening was feeling great.

"Great," he said, his eyes still closed. There was no way around it: It was wonderful to have another man touch his cock. Still wonderful. Even so.

"You want to come?"

"Yes, please. Before some fucking doctor comes in."

The stroking grew faster and stronger, till all of what was left of Zack was straining upward to one immensely orgasmic point. And then it happened, everywhere—sticky, hot, life affirming.

"Fuck," said the Leatherman, "quite a load."

Zack just gasped.

"I think you made a mess," Scott said.

"I think my nurse will probably be proud of me, seeing as how he's a big old fag."

"Let me wipe you up, anyway." And he did, gently and thoroughly.

"So are you really a leatherman?"

"Nope. Not really. Not at all. It was just a job. Disappointed?"

"Not at all." Zack had only a limited idea of what leathermen were, anyway—he'd never even been into one of their bars.

"Well, listen, sexy. I should get going. Other guys to visit."

"Hey, thanks for the...personal appearance."

"My pleasure. I hope we meet again sometime."

For one long moment, their gazes collided, blue eyes and brown.

"I don't think we will," said Zack, "but thanks."

But Zack, contrary to expectations, didn't die. It was, in fact, just the slightest bit disconcerting to have an ongoing lifetime to deal with, though at least he hadn't—unlike other HIV-positive men he knew—spent all his savings and gone deeply into debt. He was, no doubt about it, one of the lucky ones. As each antiviral drug was superseded by another, more effective one, he responded well to them all. A good diet and gym time helped, too, and he became healthy enough to work again and pretty much pick up where he'd left off.

Somewhere along the line, he acquired all the Village People's albums, even though Scott hadn't actually sung on any of them. He even found himself getting misty-eyed the first time he heard the Pet Shop Boys cover "Go West."

And he acquired something else, too: chaps, a biker cap, and a black leather jacket. Zack had, in fact, become a leatherman. Not just the dress-up type, but a living, breathing, tie-me-up-and-beat-me-hard leatherguy.

In the beginning, it had just been a matter of getting an exploratory spanking from a man who had been his almost-boyfriend for a few months. When that proved startlingly thrilling, he went further afield searching for thrills—and he found them. Aplenty.

Back when he'd been vanilla, he'd always found the leather scene to be kind of forbidding. But it wasn't particularly tough to work his way into it. *It would probably be tougher,* he thought, *to become a construction worker or a cop. Definitely tougher to become a Native American.*

Within a matter of months, he'd gone from leather wannabe to a fairly experienced player who found himself in demand at the play parties he'd begun attending, thanks to a referral from a suburban master with a nicely equipped dungeon hidden away in his garage. His popularity was in part due to his being a physically attractive guy—he knew he looked good, why deny it? But he discovered that the leather scene valued other things besides looks: aptitude, openness, and, in the case of bottoms, a willingness to suffer for the master du jour. And all those things, Zack figured, he possessed.

So while other bottoms—a goodly number of them younger, buffer, more handsome than he—were standing around the dungeon like masochistic wallflowers, Zack would be shackled to a bondage board, his naked body being tortured with a riding crop or a quirt, having the time of his life.

At about that time, he realized that wearing a T-shirt and jeans, though it wouldn't get him expelled from the fun, was no longer enough. He wanted to play dress-up, like the big boys, and began, despite limited resources, assembling black cowhide gear. "Always buy quality," his mother had taught him. "It's cheaper in the long run." And so he started patronizing the premiere local leather shop, especially enjoying the hands-on treatment the cute young clerk gave him during fittings.

Thus properly attired, Zack began an affair with a leathermaster, a man twenty years his senior who had a PhD in Buddhist studies, a tremendous dick, and a toy bag the size of Minnesota. Out of said satchel, the master would draw a delightful array of bondage gimcracks, a wide variety of pain-producing implements, and an electrical TENS unit that Zack had refused to have used on him...so far. It was hardly a long-term Master/slave relationship—Zack was discovering that, at least in his little corner of the leather world, those were considerably rarer than mythology would have it. Regardless, when he played with Master Maitland, the most extraordinary things could happen.

It wasn't just a matter of endorphins or orgasms. For Zack, bottoming for a skilled sadist often verged on a—well, at the risk of seeming foo-foo—a spiritual experience. And if Master Maitland was of the school that held that S/M play and genital sexuality didn't mix, well, that was no great problem for Zack. After a long night tied down to the rack, he would huddle under the covers of his bed and masturbate until the semen flowed. It was lovely.

The arrangement that Zack had with Master Maitland wasn't an exclusive one; actually, the idea of his actually becoming a wholly owned soi-disant "slave" seemed both silly and scary. And when Master Maitland took off on a monthlong pilgrimage to North India and Tibet, Zack found himself all dressed up with no one to submit to. So, with just the slightest bit of trepidation, he headed out to the monthly leather party at a dungeon downtown, a get-together that had become his favorite, since it provided a convenient venue for him to haul in Master Maitland's toy bag, assume the position, and be used and abused in front of an admiring knot of spectators, both friends and strangers.

The dungeon smelled, as per usual, of sweat, leather polish, and lust. There on his own, he allowed himself to lean up against a wall and survey the scene: a guy with a dozen clothespins on his dick; a blindfolded fellow suspended from a hook in the ceiling; two young men tied together face-to-face being spanked by two tops, hard. It would have been difficult to describe, to those not in the know, the exact tenor of the scene. Camaraderie mixed with torture, and there was a heavy-duty veneer of self-aware masculinity, some of it simple and genuine, some—Zack knew—carefully assumed for the evening. It felt, oddly enough, like home.

Master Maitland was, if not strictly Old Guard, Old Guardish. Zack, perhaps still the arriviste, was a lot more relaxed about dress codes, behavioral niceties, and the like. But even he looked askance at a new arrival, someone he'd never seen before, a long-haired young man striding through the half-lit dungeon in a puffy white pirate shirt, a black leather jockstrap, and—in place of regulation boots—black Converse All-Stars. Zack was, in fact, a little surprised the guy had made it past the doorman. But then, the staff was mostly volunteers, some more vulnerable than others to the appeal of a beautiful face. And it was, after all, the twenty-first century....

The handsome fellow was headed his way, and Zack guiltily noticed his sartorial disapproval being overcome by a rising sense of sexual excitement. The young man—he couldn't have been older than twenty-five—approached Zack with pleasing reticence. When he was within a few paces, he cast his eyes downward, bowed his head, and said, "Hello, Sir." He had the face, Zack thought, of a dissolute elf.

Zack scowled and nodded, the very essence of Macho Man. "Show me your ass, boy," he kind of growled, because that's the sort of thing that was expected, and because being commanded to do that particular thing always thrilled *him*. The boy turned around. He had thick thighs, a beautifully meaty butt, and, when he bent over, a perfect pink asshole nestled in dirty-blond fur. For a moment, Zack regretted not being a top.

"Enough."

The boy turned back around, and stood there looking prettily expectant.

Oh, well, any perverted port in a storm. "Suck my dick," Zack commanded. Anyway, he *hoped* it sounded like a command.

Elfboy dropped to his knees and unbuttoned Zack's Levi's. When Zack's hard cock was liberated, the boy held on to the smooth leather thighs of Zack's chaps and expertly maneuvered the erection into his mouth. The kid was a good cocksucker, no doubt about it. Zack grabbed a handful of the kneeling boy's hair and roughly guided the mouth-with-a-guy-attached back and forth over his dick till there was drool and sputtering. Even if Zack wasn't going to be abused this evening, he could still enjoy himself. He put his hands behind his head, taking care not to knock off his black leather motorcycle cap, and leaned back against the rough wall as the not-quite-leatherboy continued to worship his magnificent—that was an admirer's word, not his—meat.

And that's when he saw him, across the dungeon. Scott Stein. It had to be him. The pinch-hitting Village Person who had, at the absolute nadir of Zack's life, lent a healing hand. Plus some years, of course, and a trimmed goatee. And maybe a few pounds—one of the nice things about the real leather community was that experience and daring were as prized as youth and bodily perfection. But it was him, no doubt about it.

Okay, he dimly remembered that Stein had been a singer and a dancer, but not—except onstage—a leatherman. But back then, neither was Zack.

"Enough," Zack said. "Back off." The boy reluctantly let Zack's cock slip out of his mouth.

Zack stared at the prepossessed vision standing in the gloom. The man was, obviously, cruising. But something about him said neither, "I'm desperate enough to take whatever comes along," nor "I'm just too good for the likes of you." Instead, he seemed to be patiently waiting—and here Zack had to admit that he might be projecting—for the right bottom to present himself, confident that he would.

Zack put away his cock and headed in Stein's direction. He did his best to keep his pace measured; it wouldn't do to rush headlong like some horny teenager, but neither did he want anyone else to beat him to the punch. Finally, after what seemed like minutes, Zack was within a few feet of Stein. The erstwhile Village Person looked even more magnificent up close, the added pounds and years wearing well. And his clothing was stunning, not just the usual uniform, but a gleaming outfit, dark as night, that looked as if it might be custom made. The man's short-sleeved, button-up leather shirt was perfectly tapered, emphasizing broad shoulders, then nipping in at the waist. The top two buttons, undone, gave a glimpse of an enticingly furry chest, and tattoo dragons curled around his muscular forearms. His pants were like a second skin; a dark, dark one with ash-gray stripes running up the sides. Clipped to the man's broad, studded belt was a flogger, one of the most gorgeous floggers Zack had ever seen, its handle intricately hand-braided in black and blue—a nice visual pun, that—its tails broad and soft and just lethal-looking enough. The flogger hung against the man's left thigh, which was, for Zack, the right side, the correct side. The top side.

The man's hands were tightly encased in thin leather gloves. And his boots...ah, his boots. Knee-high Dehner motorcycle-patrolman's boots with Bal-laced insteps, the calfskin polished to a perfect sheen. They made Zack want to drop to his knees then and there. Instead he stood gazing, as non-presumptuously as possible, in Stein's direction, until he received a glance in return, then an approving nod. Zack's cock, which had largely deflated since it had left the boy's wet mouth, now surged back to full hardness and started pounding in his jeans.

He stepped forward till he was within feet of the handsome, bearded man, then waited, his head bowed, staring hungrily at the lacing of the boots. "How you doin'?" Stein said at last.

"Very well, Sir, thank you." Should he mention the time, long ago, when they'd met at Zack's not-quite-deathbed? No, he shouldn't. Either Stein wouldn't remember him at all, which would be disappointing but understandable, considering how many AIDS patients he must have visited, back in the day. Or he *would* remember, and right off, the conversation would take a turn toward the depressing. Better to wait. Wait. "But, if you'll forgive me for saying so, Sir, I could be doing better."

In a few moments, Zack was naked except for engineer boots and thick woolen socks, his wrists and ankles in restraints that were bound to a St. Andrew's cross, his back and ass exposed, vulnerable, his stiff penis perilously close to the *X*-shaped structure's rough wood.

The first few strokes of the flogger were gentle, almost soothing. Zack relaxed into the moment; Stein obviously knew what he was doing. He might not have been a bona fide leatherman in the old days, but times had clearly changed. Little by little, the blows to Zack's shoulders came harder, faster, Stein establishing a perfect rhythm, then ramping up the intensity. The sensations sometimes approached what was generally thought of as pain, but Zack had learned to process such feelings, to enjoy them, to want more. And then came the flow of endorphins, the flood of bliss. He was not a religious man, but Zack could understand why, when leathermen spoke of their experiences, they often did so in spiritual terms. He was swept away in waves of darkness, of light, of the imagined anthemic strains of "Go West." And he was grateful, so grateful. To the universe, of course, for bringing him to this moment. But specifically thankful to Scott Stein, too, for bringing him back to life in that long-ago hospital room. And for bringing him to *more* life, right here, right now. Full circle. Things were going in circles. Bright, shining circles.

And still the flogging continued. Every once in a while, Stein would switch tactics, administering sideways blows to Zack's naked, quivering ass, but always returning to work on the shoulders and upper back. Zack's flesh had become fire, his soul a flame. Or something. And still, uninvited, nonetheless goofily welcome, disco music flooded his brain, keeping crazy time with the blows to his flesh.

Fuck, his life was *amazing.*

But all good things—even perfect floggings—must come to an end. The blows slowed, softened, and eventually faded to nothing. The man behind him stroked him, leather gloves against tenderized flesh. Then, kisses, the glorious feeling of soft, wet lips, the slight tickling of a mustache—Zack had forgotten that Stein had facial hair, but of course he had. And then the kissing stopped, and Zack was enfolded from behind in the master's strong arms, the man's leather pressed up against his naked flesh.

"We're done," said the man.

Zack, who had not spoken once since the flogging had begun, said, "Thank you, Sir. Thank you so very, very much."

As his ankles and wrists were released, Zack looked around the room. Yes, he was still on Planet Earth, back in the familiar old space/time continuum, hurtling through the universe in the company of other twisted, horny men.

"Sir?"

"Yes?"

"Sir, I'm still hard. Permission to make myself come, Sir?" The leatherman had already told Zack, during negotiations, that for him, scenes were all about power and pain, not genital sexuality. But Zack also knew that he just fucking had to come. If possible.

"Granted."

So Zack reached down and, with a few short strokes, made himself shoot, his cum dripping down onto the dungeon's stained floor. It was less a cataclysmic orgasm than a long-sought release, but no less sweeter for that.

"I thought you were never going to get enough," Stein said.

Zack knew that if he said, "Actually, I didn't," it would likely sound whiny rather than complimentary. So he smiled and said, "I don't think you could ever give me too much, Sir."

The man smiled for the first time, as far as Zack knew, that evening. It was a good smile—secure, friendly—that in no way compromised the leather top's sadistic masculinity.

"So…" This was as good a time as any, Zack figured. "We've met before."

"Have we? Where?"

"In the hospital. You were visiting the AIDS ward, and you jacked me off."

"I don't think so."

"What?" Zack was genuinely confused.

"No, I mean it."

"So you weren't a member of the Village People?"

"You're kidding, right?"

Silence.

"Afraid not. You must have me confused with someone else. Really."

"Sorry," Zack said, abashed. "Sorry."

"You disappointed?"

Zack hesitated. Was he, in fact, disappointed?

A long, long moment passed before he shook his head.

SHARKSKIN

Colin Penpank

A crowded and smoky bar on a Friday night. A "neighborhood bar," which really meant it hosted all types of guys from all parts of the city. I was with my friend Larry, who was looking for husband candidates. Now on his third beer, he was in high spirits, and we hadn't even been there an hour.

"I'm in the mood for storybook romance," he said, making his hundredth scan of the room. "Hearts and flowers. Chocolates by messenger."

"Good luck." I was pretty cynical about love. In my experience, it was all slammed doors and emptied closets.

Larry set his sights on a tall blond boy, cute enough, but too animated for my taste. "*He'd* succumb to courtship," Larry observed. "One two-star dinner would do it."

"*And* a Platinum American Express card."

"You think?" he asked pensively. Larry felt he could only hold a guy with a constant shower of gifts. He was so wrong.

We lost sight of the blond boy as the crowd parted for a new arrival. The new guy moved like a shark swimming through a crowded aquarium. Everyone stepped aside.

Jeans, T-shirt, and a scuffed-up, black leather jacket. Upturned collar. Standard tough-guy drag. But it wasn't his outfit that spooked the boys. It was his pockmarked skin. His features weren't bad, but he had the most acne-scarred face I'd ever seen.

For Larry, this was malevolence incarnate, some red-hot rage that had bubbled to the surface. He turned to me.

"Feel like a beating?" he asked.

I watched the shark swim off into the dark. "It's all a show," I said. "Defensive."

"I wouldn't be too sure," said Larry. "That's a slice an' dicer if ever I saw one. You'll end up dead in bed minus a head."

I put my drink down. "I'm going for it. He's a poor little puddytat." Larry raised his eyebrows. He was worried about me, worried I'd put myself in jeopardy. He knew about my weakness for bad skin.

The weakness was almost a fetish, a holdover from my first high school crush, a beautiful but shy boy whose face was all red blotches. For most kids, acne was revolting. For me, it became just icing on a cake. I thought it meant a desire for—but fear of—sex with guys. Unfortunately, my theory never got put to the test. What I did get was a lifelong tingle whenever I was reminded of him by some poor guy's bad complexion.

I threaded my way through the crowd and found him leaning against a wall in a dark corner. What little light there was accentuated his skin's rough texture. He was alone. The shark had scared everybody off.

I leaned on the wall beside him, my shoulder touching his. We were just about the same height. The cold of the chains and cock ring hung on his black cowhide jacket went right through my shirt. We were looking out into the crowd, seeing nothing. I turned my body to face his, the better to study him. He turned his head and looked me in the eyes. Bold as brass. Both of us.

"I'm wondering if you're as mean as you look," I said. I'd had a couple of drinks, too, and couldn't quite stifle a smirk. He looked at me hard.

"What?" He was stalling for time. I was right. He *was* a puddytat.

"You heard me."

"Yeah. But I don't know what you mean."

"Yes, you do."

He gave me a cold, hard look. Maybe he didn't like my attitude. Maybe he did. Or maybe he didn't like my looks. He was deciding.

Finally he put out his hand. "Jon."

I took it. "Mark." He didn't let go. Instead he let his hand travel up my forearm. My hand traveled up along his. We squeezed. The voltage shocked the smirk off my face.

He looked back out to the crowd. "You ready to go?" he asked.

"I'll get my coat." We slowly let go of each other. He headed back through the crowd. Again, it seemed to part before him. I followed in his wake, but detoured over to the bar. Grabbing my denim jacket off the stool, I leaned into Larry's ear.

"I'm going home with Scarface."

"If you turn up dead, can I have the Warhol?"

I laughed. "Make me breakfast tomorrow. I can meet your new husband."

"Uh-huh," he said, inflecting as much disapproval as he could. Soulless-looking leather boys really scared him.

I pushed my way through the crowd to catch up with Jon,

who was already out the door. As I pulled on my jacket, I watched him zip himself into his tight cycle gear.

"I'm just a couple blocks," he said.

"Fine." We started off, walking briskly to counter the chill of the fall night. When we passed under the streetlights, I could see my breath. We walked in silence for a block or so until he gave me a sideways look.

"So," he said, "you a model?"

"Actor."

"You look familiar."

"Commercials. Soaps. And you?"

"And me what? I'm *not* a model." He gave a little grimace. "I teach."

"Oh, cool. What?"

"Math. Catholic girls' school."

"Jeez. Ouch."

"Exactly." We were at his place, a small brick house with a wide front porch.

"You live by yourself?" I asked.

"Yep," he said as he unlocked the door and pushed it in. When he turned on the lamps, a teacher's home came into view. Polished wood floors. A Morris chair. Bookcases, framed old maps.

"Beer?" he asked, as he made his way into the house.

"Not for me. Water, maybe." Actually, I was parched. I'd been drinking gin. I followed him down the hall that led to the kitchen. It was the first time I got a good look at his whole body. I liked what I saw. He still had that snug leather jacket on. That sexy black leather jacket that barely met the top of his tight, beltless jeans.

After he handed me my glass, he clinked his beer bottle against it.

"Here's lookin' at *you*, kid." He smiled. Nice smile. Then it clicked. Bogart's skin had been rough, too.

"Into movies?" I asked.

"Big-time. Done any?

"Nope. Someday. If I'm lucky. Maybe a movie of the week, that kind of thing."

"What, no Scorsese? No Spielberg?"

"Not a chance in hell."

"No?"

"Too pretty." He looked surprised. "Dime a dozen."

"Oh. Really."

"Nature of the biz. They pigeonhole you by your look."

"Like you did with me?" He looked down at the floor quickly. Was he blushing?

I put my glass down and took the beer out of his hand, setting it on the counter. I grabbed the bottom of his leather jacket and pulled him close to me.

He swallowed hard, still looking at the floor.

"You are really, really, *really* beautiful," he said quietly. I knew what he was thinking: *Why me?*

I reached up and pulled his head back, looking at the rough skin up close. "I love *your* looks." I felt his ragged cheek with my fingertips.

He shot me a sharp glare, grabbed my wrist and yanked my hand down. I watched him realize what it was all about. His eyes glistened. He just looked at me awhile. Then he let go of my wrist, put his arms around me, and gave a squeeze. He nuzzled his sandpaper cheek against my face. I might have heard a sigh.

"Ya know," I said softly, "actors role-play."

"They do, don't they?"

"And they're usually pretty good at it." He pulled away from me far enough to look into my eyes. He studied them for a moment.

"Got any kinks?" he asked.

Even though my fetish is common, it has such power over me I'm always reluctant to reveal it. He watched me, waiting to hear something true.

"I was a swimmer," I said.

"Gotcha."

"And you?"

"I really like hand jobs."

"Okay." Hand jobs turned me into a schoolboy. A *bad* schoolboy.

"And I need to be restrained. I need to have my hands tied behind my back. Otherwise I'll come."

"Say again?"

"I can't come," he said. "I want *you* to come, but I can't. It hurts if I do. It's a condition."

This was something new. In fact it was stunningly new. This might be the exact opposite of my usual experience. Guys always come too fast with me. Sometimes I just pull off my shirt, they take a look, they squirt.

He broke away. "Just don't let me come. Is that okay?"

I smiled.

"C'mon," he said. He went down the hall into a bedroom. "I've got something *like* a Speedo, but maybe you'd prefer these...." I leaned on the doorframe while he pulled open drawers and rummaged through them like a madman. I started to think. Something other than a Speedo would be safer. Gin plus a Speedo plus bad skin plus tied up would equal me out of control. Way out of control.

Finally he found what he was looking for. He held up a pair of jet black leather briefs with lace-up sides. My heart started racing. I was instantly hard. *And there's the cherry on top,* I thought.

"They'll do," I was able to choke out. He began tearing off his clothes.

"Go into the living room. I'll come in. There's a drawer in the side table."

I went into the living room and opened the drawer. Magazines. Remote controls. And a three-foot length of braided twine made into a rough, prickly rope. I sat down in the Morris chair, took off my jacket and shirt, and undid the top buttons of my jeans. I turned off all but one of the lamps.

He crept into the dim room slowly, stepping into the one remaining pool of light. He raised his arms and put himself on display. Slowly he turned around full circle, like some runway model.

He had a striking, natural build. I should have known. With that scarred-up face, it *had* to be a good body. Great legs and a musclebound ass. Probably a runner. As he slowly turned, I could see he liked showing off his body. He could shift the attention away from his face.

The almost-too-small black leather briefs were tight as a second skin. And the way they cupped all but the bottom of his hard little ass and curved down in front to his pubes! Jesus Fucking Christ!

The capper was the wide gap on the sides where the halves of the tight shorts didn't meet. I could see his bare skin under the crisscrossed rawhide laces that held the suit together. The laces were pulled taut as could be through silvery grommets, and tied at the bottom in neat bows. The long ends ran down the sides of his muscled thighs.

I could see his boner stretched sideways under the dark leather. It took my breath away. I was hard as a rock, and had been from the moment he'd flashed that outfit at me back in the bedroom.

I picked up the braided twine and went over to him. He turned around and put his hands behind his back, letting me wrap the braid around his wrists five times before tying a stiff knot. The rope was so rough I didn't even like touching it.

"Is that *okay*? It doesn't hurt?"

"It helps," he said hoarsely.

We were both breathing heavily. There was tension. We were within a cloud of tension. I wasn't sure what I was going to do. Jon didn't know either.

He reached back and grabbed the top of my jeans, trying to get his bound hands inside. I let him fiddle a bit, but he couldn't quite manage to reach in. I ran my hands over his arms as he struggled, feeling his muscles at work. The more his triceps popped, the more excited I got.

I grabbed him by the shoulders and turned him around. I was faced with my dream. A body ready for sex. Leather briefs. A handsome face. And a ravaged complexion that humiliated him every day of his life.

What a beautiful gift. Just for me. All tied up in leather bows. I could do whatever I wanted with it.

I grabbed his pecs, pulled him close, and leaned into him as if going for a kiss. His eyes closed and his lips parted, but I didn't let our mouths meet. I stopped just short, so that he was breathing into my mouth and I was breathing into his.

Then I locked onto one corner of his upper lip and sucked on it gently. His mouth opened wider. He exhaled deeply. Our mouths came together, sucking and twisting and chewing.

He started to melt. It was time to grab his hard leather package. I squeezed his cock and balls, yanking them back and forth along with the small briefs. He yelped and fell against me, shuddering.

I pushed him back to watch myself twisting and tugging the

bulged-out leather. His eyes were wet again. He was looking me over good for the first time.

"Oh god oh god," he said quietly. He was licking up my torso with his eyes. My jeans were sagging off my butt, open nearly to my dick. His gaze was following my treasure trail, almost too dazed to take it in. I was afraid he was going to go off, just like everybody else.

"You're not going to come, are you?"

He broke his stare and looked away from me. I played with his cock under the tight cowhide, rubbing it, feeling every inch.

"I can't come," he said slowly. "Seriously. It's painful if I come."

"Then don't."

He glanced back at me, then down to my hand kneading his leather-wrapped cock. His eyes traveled back up my arm, mesmerized by the flexing my biceps made as I worked on his crotch. His body began trembling. His knees were buckling.

"Maybe this wasn't a good idea," he gasped. "I get a look at you and I'm afraid I might not hold it."

He could talk all he wanted, but nothing would get my hand off that silky leather knob unless I wanted it off. His cock seemed to grow bigger by the second.

"You want a safeword?"

"Yes...." He was starting to groan. I let go of his crotch and squeezed his waist. He looked into my eyes.

"Fuggiddaboudit." I couldn't help grinning.

"What?" He was slack-jawed.

"Don't worry," I said. "We'll just have a little fun."

I squeezed his oblique and brushed my hand lightly down over the laces. One finger poked into an opening and curved into the front of the packed little shorts. I could just barely feel the tip of his wet cock. My finger circled around and around his dick hole, helping it pump out more precum. He twisted to get away, but my arm behind his back held him in place.

"Okay, a little fun." he said. "Just don't do *that* anymore. Stop. Please. I mean it." He was being serious again. "You've got to ease up when I say so, okay?"

"No problem." I eased my finger out of the leather trunks. It was soaking wet.

I grabbed his head with both hands and held it still, tongue-kissing him over and over, quick and rough, until he could barely catch a breath.

I wanted to get into that leather-wrapped gift package. I ran my hands down his chest, squeezing each muscle that came into my grasp. But my fingers couldn't wriggle into the briefs—they were laced up too tight.

I reached around to untie one of the bows. He broke free and jumped away, almost falling.

"No! Don't! Don't!"

But it was too late. I'd held on to one end. When he pulled away, the knot came undone. The shorts loosened.

"Oh. Sorry 'bout that. Want me to tie it back?"

"*Yes.*"

I thought about it.

"In a minute." I ran my hand down his abs, jamming it into his suit and wrapping my fingers around his cock. He moaned.

"No…now," he said.

I felt like a little boy with a new toy.

"Hey! I *like* your cock. Jesus, is *it* hard." I said it like a teen on a sitcom would. He tried to collect himself, struggling against wave after wave of body tremors.

"I asked you," he said. "You've gotta get your hand out of my trunks and tie them back up." He did sound like he meant it. What an actor. Or maybe he wasn't acting. I was too hot to care.

"But Jon, I like this." I kept running my other hand up and down his rippled chest, pinching his nipples each time I found them. "It's not my fault if you come. Just hold it in." He tried to nod, and he tried not to buckle over from my fingers working his cock. I let them learn every vein, every ridge.

"I can't come," he said slowly.

"Jon. You're repeating yourself."

He looked up, incredulous. His cock was hard as a board and getting sloppy from all the precum. I love it when guys make a lot of precum. It was all over the inside of the shorts, starting to bleed through the leather, making little wet spots on the front.

Keeping his cock inside the trunks, I gripped it by the base and pulled on it sideways. I pulled on it like I was trying to pull it off of his body. He fell forward against me.

"Good boy. You're doing fine." I kept pulling on it steadily. I twisted it like I was trying to rip it off, but my hand kept slipping.

"Stop it! Stop! Stop!" he yelled. He jerked away violently, trying to break my grip. It wasn't easy to hold on to his slippery prick.

"Mark," he yelled. "You've gotta go easier!"

He was breathing deeply, rapidly, trying to calm down. "This isn't working out. You won't go easy. You're being a real ass-hole. I want you to get your hand *off* my *dick*. I want you to *untie* my hands, and I want you to get the *fuck* out of my house. Just leave. You got that? Let go!" I could feel his cock stiffen into that ready-to-shoot mode.

I let go and pulled my hand out. He collapsed to his knees, jellified. I guess I'd been holding him up by his dick. I wiped my slimy hand across his mouth, then reached under his armpits and pulled him to his feet.

"I'm sorry. I'll be more considerate. We need to take our minds off it. Here. Let's walk a little." I grabbed the front of the black shorts. My knuckles rubbed against his dick. He followed me jerkily, spitting, trying to shake the precum off his face. His breathing got more regular after a few laps around the room.

"Okay," he said.

"You need to cool off."

"I'm cooler now, wait. Let's rest. That was so fast. Christ. I wasn't ready." He gave me a look that told me he didn't understand what had happened. Had he not expected passion? That surprised me. He should have known. I'm an actor. I deal in passion. I manufacture it. I'm in the passion business.

"Don't you worry, Jon, I'm going to cool you down." I pulled him along to the front door and put my free hand on the latch.

"Ohhhh no! Don't even *think* about it! Absolutely no *fucking* way. I *mean* it, Mark!"

"What? It'll do you good." I opened the door, felt a blast of cold air, and pulled him after me.

"Shit!" He was violent, trying to backpedal into the house. But with his hands tied he couldn't hold on to anything. I wrapped my arm around his waist and threw him out onto the cold porch with a heavy thud.

As soon as we were outside he became deadly still and silent. The porch light was off but we could see clearly in the moonlight. We looked over across the street. A couple was walking by slowly, deep in conversation. They hadn't seen us. Farther down, a car was starting up. Jon was shivering and breathing heavily, each breath forming a cloud.

"Okay, you win," he whispered. "Very funny. Now take me in. Mark, I'm serious." He looked at me hard so I could tell he meant business. "I *live* here, Mark," he said, stating the obvious.

"What? You think behind those dark windows everyone is watching *Teacher* get danced around? In his teeny tiny little leather *muscleboy* trunks with the long laces?" I pushed him up against the ice-cold brick wall, rubbing him into it. "Give us a kiss."

He was already shivering. He wanted to yell. I pinned him to the wall and gave him a long, gentle, loving kiss.

"Thank you," I said softly, looking into his eyes. "You're a good guy. A decent and good guy." It was a line from my soap.

He melted again. I moved my hands back down over his chest and abs. Jesus, what a hard body, even harder now, shivering out in the cold.

On the side where the laces were almost undone, the front of his leather briefs had folded over. I saw the top of his sideways boner. The suit was so beautiful like that. I got an idea.

"Jon? Can I try these on?"

"Oh, noooo, *please*!" he pleaded.

"No? What about this?"

I reached down and popped the rest of the buttons on my fly, pulling out my hard-on. Squeezing it between the laces, I jammed it into the front of his briefs. Jon watched my cock slide under his, then his eyelids half closed and he moaned out loud. I put my hand over his mouth.

"Jon!" I whispered. "Remember where you are." I felt like laughing.

I stretched the trunks up to cover our dicks, making a big leather sausage. It was the most beautiful sight I'd ever seen: my hand clutching this little patch of wet cowhide, holding our cocks together.

I started rocking my hips ever so gently, leaning back, watching myself fucking this little leatherboy costume of his. With just a couple of strokes, his slippery cock, the wet hide, the cold metal grommets, and the pinching laces brought me to the brink. I decided to come. It would never get any better than this.

It only took a couple more deep jabs for me to shoot. I

whipped backward and then fell against him, biting into his shoulder to keep from yelling. I kept on milking my cock, jerking his at the same time, coming and coming and coming. That leather suit had to be filled up with all the cream I could make.

I finished and took a few deep breaths.

I put my hand on Jon's forehead, raised his head up, and gave him a peck on the cheek. His eyes were vacant, glazed over. His shivering body felt like a mass of hot wires, each sizzling with current.

I let his head fall back down. He watched me pull my dick out of his shorts and wipe it on the leather. I left it hanging out of my jeans, so he could see it dripping threads of cum.

"You came," he whispered. "We're done."

No. We weren't.

I reached in and got his dick in my hand. It was so hard I couldn't even squeeze it. There was so much precum I could only glide my hand back and forth, like it was on rollers. His head began to swing from side to side, keeping time with the sucking sound each jerk made.

Then we heard voices down the sidewalk.

"Stop stop stop stop!" His cock was pulsing. His body went rigid and his eyes squeezed shut. He was trying with all his might to hold back a geyser.

We heard laughing. Jon opened his eyes in terror. I could feel his cock get ready to shoot. He couldn't get any closer without coming.

I pulled him away from the wall into the shadows and braced myself so he couldn't thrash out of control. He was as stiff as rigor mortis, afraid to move, terrified of exploding.

I stopped stroking his cock and loosened my grip. The voices on the street stopped. Were they watching us? I could feel his cock jumping on its own. It felt huge, bigger than it was.

I yanked down the wet leather skin. My cum, which had pooled around his balls, slid out and hit the porch with a splat. I pulled his dick out straight toward me, pushed it down, and then let go. It smacked flat up against his hard belly, splashing jism. I grabbed his clenched little glutes with both hands and pulled him to me, sandwiching his cock between us. With every breath he took, his slippery prick slid up and down between our abs.

I leaned in, running the tip of my tongue over his rough cheek, tasting the salt. I got up close to his ear. Whispering. Turning myself into Eddie Haskell. Into every mean little punk on every show there ever was.

"Okay, *Jonny*. You big *baby*. I stopped *jagging off* your little *weenie* like you said. So if it *squirts*, and you hurt yourself, it's not *my fault*, see? It'll be *your* fault...and don't you fucking splatter any on *me*...or this little *jungleboy thing* you tie yourself into? I'll *undo it*.... I'll get ahold of it under your wet *balls* and whip it off you.... Then I'll wipe your *jism* off my *chest muscles* with it...."

His whole body was straining, squeezing down, trying to push back the coming explosion. He was failing. I could feel the cum rising in his cock as I crunched my abs on it over and over.

"Then you'll be *naked*, Jonny...and you'll be *sorry*...'cause I'll *pinch* the tip of your sloppy little *pee-pee*...to make you dribble *more* on the porch...."

His was quaking violently. I looked out into the street.

"Uh-oh.... Your *dad's* home early. Oh *man*, are you gonna get it...." I smiled and nodded to Dad. "Good *evening*, Mr. *Cleaver*."

That did it. Jon's head snapped back. All I could think was *I bet he screams*.

I went into Larry's steamed-up kitchen through the back door. I could smell coffee and maple syrup. He was making French toast. The blond husband candidate was in Larry's robe, sitting at the table, reading the paper.

Ah. Domesticity. Alive and well. Larry heard me closing the door. He looked around from the stove, spatula in hand.

"Oh, good timing," he said, rolling his eyes. "Pull up a chair. Show us your bruises."

BOOTLEGGER

Thomas Roche

Flanked by Jay and Breaker, Bad Mike frog-marched the kid upstairs from the backroom straight into Johnny's office, finding the big man tucked behind his desk, waiting for them. The kid came in without a fight, even though Mike had his wrists pinned in the small of his back. He was tall, lean, less fat on him than a chili dog and fries, his taut body knotted with muscle like he'd been working out every day for ten years, which he had. He was twenty-four, maybe twenty-five, poured into a pair of skintight leather pants and a sleeveless white T-shirt, buckled into a heavy pair of engineer boots. His hair was close-cropped high and tight above the ears, two days into a beard, his chiseled looks brought out nice and hard by what could have been a Vandyke if he'd put a little work into it.

Mike stood the kid up and held his wrists pinned behind him easily in one hand, the other hand cinched on the kid's shoulder. The punk glanced back with a sneer as if to say he could break free if he wanted, only he didn't, and Mike scowled back as if to say, No you couldn't, fucker, no you fucking well couldn't.

The leather bar's upstairs office was furnished in Late Post-Sleaze, with a soiled old couch and a shredded armchair, and near the window a kneeling bench with leather-padded arms outstretched. Johnny had his big boots on the desk, a stogie in his hand. He slowly brought the cigar up to his bearded mouth and puffed a little, his face expressionless between the dark beard and the famous leather cap.

"What's the story?" growled Johnny.

"Bootlegger," Bad Mike answered. "Says his name's Blackie. Caught him trying to hustle tricks in the backroom; says he's a top. I asked around—he's been doing the cheapskates in the QuikMotel down the road for a Franklin and a joint or two, maybe some bourbon. Course he denies it."

"Hey," said the kid, grinning. "I didn't deny nothin'."

Bad Mike jerked his wrists and growled fiercely, and said, "Now you're gonna change your story? Confess to the big man and make me look bad, motherfucker?"

It all happened quick—the kid went spinning, got his wrists free, clocked Bad Mike before Breaker and Jay could grab him. Mike just stood there and took it, uttering an involuntary "Uh!" as the blow connected. The two goons got the kid, one wrist each, and held him while he tried to kick. Breaker took over from there and held both the hustler's wrists, spinning him around to face Johnny again while Bad Mike reached out and grabbed the kid's hair. There was barely enough to grab, but Bad Mike managed it; you could call it a talent.

Jay stood leaning up against the doorjamb, picking his nails and watching the scene unfold—his lack of concern was legendary.

Johnny looked the kid up and down, appraising the look that'd come into those baby-blue eyes: fear, just a little, but plenty to work with. Johnny's lips twisted into something sort of, but not a lot, like a smile.

Johnny pointed across the desk with his stogie.

"Two things I don't like about you, kid—what'd you say your name was?"

"Blackie," the kid snapped before Bad Mike could spit it out. Mike scowled; knowing Johnny would forget, he'd already practiced the contempt with which he'd repeat the little fucker's name. "Name's Blackie. Ask around, Johnny, they'll all tell you: I do them right, leave 'em smiling." He sniggered. "Walking funny, but smiling."

Johnny stared hard for what seemed like a long time, the five seconds of aching silence painful to everyone except maybe Johnny. Slowly, he brought the cigar back to his mouth and inserted it.

"Make that three things," he finally said, talking around the butt. "Four, actually. And they all come down to disrespect." The kid went to say something, but Johnny's glare froze him. "First, it's disrespectful to turn tricks in my joint when you don't work for me. Second, it's bad juju to slap the help around unless I tell you to. Then there's numbers three and four: Don't call me Johnny, punk, you call me 'Sir' until instructed otherwise. And last…who the fuck told you I felt like hearing you brag?"

Blackie chuckled, struggling lightly against Breaker's hands on his wrists and Bad Mike's hand in his hair. He said it with a sneer: "Sorry, *Sir*, didn't mean no disrespect. But a guy's got to make a living, and I figured…you know, it ain't no secret what goes on upstairs here. I figure maybe you could use a new hand. I swing a mean one, *Sir*." The contempt with which Blackie managed to infuse that single syllable was impressive.

Johnny pushed back his cracked-leather office chair and stood slowly. He put the stogie in an ashtray and let it burn as he came out from behind the desk. As Johnny approached, Breaker and Bad Mike turned to keep the kid facing the big man. Johnny came up so close that the four men could smell each other. He wrapped one big hand around the kid's throat, not enough to choke him, just enough to let him know it was there. Johnny had about two inches on the kid, two inches and thirty pounds of muscle. Packed into his own leather pants, Johnny wore a wife-beater that showed off his tatts: USMC, MOTHER, OUTLAW.

Johnny fixed the kid's eyes in his, saw what he wanted.

"This your idea of a job application?"

The kid shrugged almost imperceptibly. The fear in his eyes had coalesced, but he was doing a pretty good job of hiding it. Too bad for him Johnny was an expert at finding it.

Blackie said: "I do okay hustling on my own. But yeah, if you want I could, you know, audition. I swing a mean one."

"So you said. What is it you swing, kid?"

Again, the imperceptible shrug, the coalescing of fear as Johnny leaned close, smelled the bourbon on the kid's breath.

"Floggers, singletails, paddles. My hand, if the trick isn't strapped. I ain't got my own gear yet, so I borrow. Loan me a flogger, we'll see what I can do to Mr. Glassjaw here." He sniggered again, and Bad Mike pulled the kid's hair.

Johnny's free hand came up and grabbed the punk's crotch, swollen behind the skintight leather jeans. He looked deep into the kid's eyes and grinned behind his dark beard.

"Hell, yeah, I'll audition you," said Johnny. "Jay, get me a flogger. Bullhide."

"Be right back, Chief." Jay disappeared through the soiled doorway while Johnny felt the punk up. He could feel the kid stiffening under the leather.

One hand on Blackie's throat, the other on his crotch, Johnny said: "You proud of this package?"

Again the kid shrugged. "It pays the rent."

"How about that smart fuckin' mouth?" asked Johnny. "It pay the rent, too?"

"I ain't Tom Brokaw if that's what you mean," growled Blackie with a scowl. "I don't swing that way."

Johnny leaned close, brought his hand up, ran his fingers over Blackie's plump lips.

"Yeah, we'll see," he said, just as Jay came back with the flogger, and Johnny nodded to Breaker and Bad Mike.

As the two thugs wrestled him onto the bench, it hit Blackie hard just how it was going to go down upstairs at Johnny's place. His muscles went taut against them but Breaker and Bad Mike held fast, forcing his arms up against the padding of the kneeling bench just as Blackie's leather-clad knees hit the well-worn surface underneath. Blackie started to laugh.

"I get it, start at the bottom, that it, Johnny? I already told you I don't swing that way; now you're gonna see if you can crack me, huh? Be my guest."

Bad Mike and Breaker got the straps around Blackie's arms and ankles, as Johnny retrieved his stogie, took a puff, and accepted the flogger from Jay.

He made a few slashes through the air, leaning forward to watch the way Blackie's skin goose-bumped as it got a whiff of the wind from those passing fronds.

"You'd be a lot more convincing if your voice wasn't shaking," said Johnny, and even with the punk facing away from him it was obvious that Blackie had heard it shake—though Johnny hadn't. It was a bluff, but a damn good one.

Jay'd fished out his switch and clicked it open; he grabbed the kid's neckline and drew the switch down the white cotton, blade so sharp it didn't even make a ripping sound. Bad Mike and Breaker backed off. Blackie squirmed as he felt his shirt going away and then opened his mouth as if to say something. Johnny hoisted the whip and smiled.

Hearing the flogger's tails swish backward, Blackie blurted: "Wh-what do I get if I make it?"

Johnny chuckled.

He said: "A hand job—what do you think?" and brought the whip down.

Upstairs at Johnny's place there was no such thing as a warm-up. The bullhide flogger was heavy enough to open flesh, but Johnny wasn't quite that kind of top. The punk had just enough muscle to make things interesting, and Johnny laid into him with a savage pleasure that doubled when he saw the kid's lithe frame twist under the first half-dozen strokes. Blackie took it like a chieftain, first pressing his lips together and then gritting his teeth. He tried to look away so Johnny wouldn't see it, which was too bad for Blackie since there was a mirror in front of the kneeling bench. Not only could Johnny see him struggling to take it, the kid had to look at himself.

He responded by closing his eyes, but another dozen strokes into it they were wide open, his mouth a spacious O as he fought not to make strangling sounds.

Johnny finally got those sounds just a few strokes later, and the way the kid was surging against his straps made the big man want to take a break—not for Blackie's sake, but for his own. He handed the whip to Jay and knelt down beside the kneeling bench.

There was the tender feeling of the rising whip welts, yeah, as Johnny drew his fingers gently over the punk's marked back. That had Johnny nice and hard, but that's not what really did it for him. What did it for him was what he found when he slid his hand down between the punk's leather-clad thighs and reached around—not like he hadn't known it'd be there, but still. Every fresh one's like a new discovery, and here there was plenty to discover.

Blackie squirmed slightly as Johnny felt it, measured it with his hand, slapped it a little. He shut his eyes tight so he wouldn't have to look at Johnny, wouldn't have to look at himself in the big mirror that showed Johnny every contour of the punk's smug face giving way to the surge in his crotch.

With his free hand, Johnny grabbed the punk's short hair. "Open your eyes," he growled.

Blackie didn't, and Johnny pulled and squeezed—hard on the hair, firm on the cock. The punk opened his eyes and looked at himself as Johnny unzipped the leather pants and took out Blackie's dick.

There wasn't a whisper of underwear, of course, not even a jockstrap. Blackie was hung, you had to grant him that. Johnny pulled back Blackie's foreskin and rubbed the head with his fingertips: wet and drooling. Johnny wrapped his hand around the middle of the shaft and began to pump.

Blackie let out a strangled yelp, then a long, low moan. He wasn't far off; in the mirror, Johnny saw a glistening stream of precum dribble off and streak down to the carpet.

Blackie started to relax in his bonds, and his hips began to move in time with Johnny's strokes. He stopped resisting, and when he closed his eyes again it was because he was lost in the sensation, not because he was trying to look away. Johnny jerked the punk's head again and growled at him to open. Blackie did, and watched himself as his eyes glazed over.

Johnny backed off at the last moment, leaving the kid panting and hungry. He got the whip back from Jay and twirled it, listening to Blackie moan as he anticipated the next stroke. Johnny made him wait for it, as long as he could stand. Then he drew the whip across the punk's back and watched his hips surge forward, the kneeling bench thundering and groaning as the muscled body strained against it.

Blackie shot his load on the fifth or sixth stroke, slicking up the bench, the floor, and the mirror. As he came, he let out a roaring yell of desperation, like he was giving it up, finally—an orgasm he'd been saving up for since the first time he'd swung a whip.

Johnny finished the little shit's punishment and went back to kneel against him again, grabbing his hair and making him open his eyes and look into the mirror as he peeled back the foreskin and rubbed the head of his softening cock—so gentle, yet still so hard it hurt.

When Blackie went slack on the bench and his cock finally went down all the way, Johnny stood up, wiped his hand in the punk's hair, and nodded at Jay.

Johnny growled: "Get this little piggy bottom a jockstrap and some combat boots. Let's put him on bar number three, see if he can bring 'em in bottoming as fast as he has pretending to be a top."

He grabbed Blackie's hair, now moist with sweat and cum. Blackie's eyes were glazed more than ever now, and when Johnny looked at them in the mirror, the punk met his gaze, then lowered his eyes.

"You'll get to top again," smiled Johnny. "Some day. If you still want to...but I'm betting you won't. Meantime, make your new boss proud."

Frog-marched by Bad Mike, the kid went out without a fight, panting.

CAPTURE, TEST, AND SELL

Christopher Pierce

Curtis looked out at the sea of leather and flesh and smiled contentedly.

The gay leather street fair was an annual event, something Curtis looked forward to all year.

He was a hunter, and these were his favorite hunting grounds. He knew he blended in easily—he was not terribly tall, more stocky than muscular, with decent looks but not model handsome. He was shirtless, a leather harness accentuating his hairy chest, tight jeans showing off his sizable package, nice black boots on his feet. His skin was tanned dark, with some modern-primitive tattoos decorating his arms. With his high-and-tight haircut and trimmed mustache and goatee, Curtis looked like any other early-forties leatherman out for a good time at the fair.

But unlike the other men, Curtis was there for more than fun and fucking. He was looking for prey, and he knew he would find it. Leathermen and their admirers came from all over the country to attend the event, hundreds of them. The fair was one of the few places he could hunt in public without being detected.

The hunter stood in the shadows, watching the men as they examined merchandise at vendors' booths and cruised each other, hoping to hook up. His eyes scanned the crowd, searching for potential prey.

And there he was.

A young man in his early twenties, with brown eyes and short auburn hair, walked slowly by. He looked like Good Prey: he was alone, and as he looked around, taking it all in, his wide eyes showed he was new to the scene.

The hunter followed the young man as he slowly worked his way through the throng. Falling into step behind him, Curtis admired the guy's butt, clearly outlined inside his tight cutoff jeans. The young man's leather boots were shiny and new, probably purchased just for this event. Decently developed arms protruded from a white T-shirt framed by a nice new leather vest.

It was time to move in.

Curtis stepped up behind the young man and deliberately bumped him. The guy stumbled forward, but the hunter grabbed him before he could fall onto the rough pavement.

"Fuck!" the young man said, twisting around to face the hunter. "What are you...?"

"Shit, man, I'm so sorry!" Curtis said. The guy's face was cute and innocent, the face of prey. "I didn't mean to bump you like that—will you accept my apology if I buy you a beer?"

The hunter watched his prey's eyes rove over his muscled arms, hairy chest, and bulging crotch. *He's mine,* Curtis thought. The young man smiled, showing perfect white teeth.

"Sure," he said, "that'd be great." The hunter put a firm hand on the guy's shoulder.

"Wait here," Curtis said, "I'll be right back."

The prey nodded agreement, and the hunter worked his way through the crowd to the nearest concession stand. He bought a beer and walked to a spot on the side of the street where he could turn his back to the crowds. He took a tiny vial of ash-gray powder from his pocket and twisted off the top. The hunter emptied the powder into the beer and waited while it dissolved. The empty vial went back into the pocket, and Curtis headed back to where the young man was watching the crowd with wonder.

He grinned at the older man, obviously glad he was back.

"Here you go," the hunter said, handing his prey the beer.

"Thank you, Sir," the young man said.

"What's your name?"

"Casey, Sir."

"Cute name, cute guy."

The young man blushed.

"Aren't you having anything?" he asked the hunter.

"I'll have something later," Curtis said. "You go ahead."

"Okay," Casey said, then lifted his beer to his lips and drank deeply. Almost instantly his eyes grew unfocused. He shook his head, trying to clear it.

"I feel funny," he said. His grip on the beer loosened, and Curtis grabbed the bottle before it could crash on the pavement. Casey staggered forward a step, his knees shaking.

"I…" he started to say, but his eyes closed and he started to fall. In one smooth movement, the hunter caught him and leaned down, letting the young man collapse over his right shoulder. Then he stood up and tossed the beer bottle in a trash bin. With the boy on his shoulder, Curtis started to work his way through the crowd. He had a long walk back to his hotel. The sight of the hunter, carrying his unconscious prey, elicited a variety of responses from other men.

Some of them laughed at Casey, and Curtis understood why. It was distinctly undignified to be carried over another man's shoulder, ass in the air, torso, arms, and head dangling uselessly upside down behind the bearer's back.

"Your friend have too much to drink?"

Curtis grinned and nodded when anyone asked this. This was one of the reasons he loved hunting at the leather fair: one man carrying another was not all that unusual a sight. There were many possible reasons for him to be hauling Casey, and the hunter just said "Yeah" to every question he was asked.

"Your friend have too much to drink?"

"Yeah."

"Sunstroke got the best of him?"

"Yeah."

"Too tired to walk?"

"Yeah."

Men who thought of themselves as dominant took one look at Curtis and his burden and nodded with approval: they figured the hot leather daddy had secured himself a submissive boytoy for the afternoon. These tops usually said something like "Gotta get me some of *that!*" and slapped Casey's ass. Curtis would tighten his grip on his prey's legs, hefting him slightly higher over his shoulder, and, just to make sure there was no confusion, say, "He's mine." The men were not wrong in their assumption that Curtis was going to use this guy sexually. They just didn't know how the encounter would end: with Curtis selling the young man for a very high price. A few guys, probably drunk themselves, tried to pull Casey down, but when the hunter snarled at them, they gave up.

Curtis liked carrying his prey. It felt primal. He'd captured this man, taken ownership of him. He enjoyed jostling Casey around on his shoulder, readjusting him, knowing that the guy wouldn't wake up from the knockout drug for at least another hour. That gave him plenty of time. Plenty.

But as sexy as it was, intellectually and physically, to have captured the young man, and despite Casey's moderate weight and the hunter's strength and stamina, carrying his prey's dead weight through a dense crowd of drinking, smoking, sweating men quickly grew tiresome. Curtis soon was looking forward to the quiet and privacy of his hotel.

In a short while, he was carrying the young man into the hotel lobby, getting hardly a glance from the staff; they'd probably seen similar things since the leather celebration had begun. Again, Curtis was thankful for the fair. Where else could he hunt in broad daylight and draw hardly a second look? He got into an empty elevator and sighed, glad to be alone at last. But just before the doors closed someone else got on, a young man wearing leather chaps, shirtless and showing off his defined chest and abs. Tired and thirsty, the hunter hoped he wouldn't have to make small talk, or to come up with any more explanations for the man slung over one shoulder.

But the new arrival said nothing, though Curtis saw his eyes dart back and forth between Casey's unconscious body and the blank elevator door. As the trim young man got off the elevator, he glanced at the hunter on his way out.

"Wish that was me," he said with a grin.

"You gonna be around tomorrow?" Curtis asked.

"Definitely."

"Then you may get your chance."

"Great!" the young man said. "Have a good afternoon, Sir."

And the doors closed behind him. The hunter rode up the remaining few floors. He was going to be glad to set his burden down. He'd been carrying him beneath the hot sun for a good twenty minutes. Curtis walked to his room, fished his key card out of his pocket, and let himself in.

First things first.

He carried Casey over to the double bed and laid him down. Then he opened his suitcase, which lay on the floor next to the bed, and pulled out a few tools. First he forced a leather gag into his prey's mouth, buckling it securely behind his head. Then he used two pairs of leather cuffs to cinch together Casey's hands at the wrists, and his feet at the ankles.

The hunter stared at his bound and gagged prey for a moment.

The guy was so damn cute. Fucking hot lying there all trussed up, his pretty face lost in drug-induced slumber. He'd looked so happy when Curtis had come back with the beer. If only he'd known what the hunter was going to do with him.

Curtis shook his head, trying to clear his thoughts.

It was not professional for a hunter to be distracted by his prey. His job was to capture, test, and sell. That was what he was going to do. But first, a shower. Satisfied that Casey was securely bound, Curtis took off his harness—the damn thing had been itching anyway—kicked off his boots, and peeled down his jeans. He took a short shower, loving the feel of the cool water as it splashed over his sun-heated skin. He fisted his cock a few times to get it hard, although, released from the tight pants, it didn't really need any help.

Refreshed, naked and aroused, the hunter returned to the bedroom. His prey hadn't moved an inch. Curtis looked at Casey for a few minutes, just enjoying the sight of him and thinking *Mine. He's all fucking mine.*

Realizing that the knockout drug would be wearing off soon, he figured it was time for the second part of a hunter's job: the test. Curtis unhooked the strap from behind Casey's head and pulled the gag gently out of the young man's mouth. Then he propped the prey up against the bed's headboard, in a sitting position. Casey remained unconscious through all this, breathing deeply as if in deep sleep. Once his prey was properly situated, the hunter climbed up on the bed and stood, bracing himself against the wall, his crotch in Casey's face. Curtis took his cock in one hand and placed it in front of the young man's mouth, then gently pushed in.

Casey's lips parted, and the hunter's dick slid nicely into his mouth. The hunter groaned softly at the pleasure that coursed through him as he did what he'd wanted to do since he first spotted his prey: fuck his mouth. The young man's tongue was soft but firm, his spit cool and smooth. Curtis savored every delicious thrust as he made love to that mouth, his dick sliding in and out. Soon the hunter felt a climax rising in him and he pulled out, not wanting the test to be over so soon. He stepped backward and got down on his knees, straddling his prey.

Then he did something unexpected, something he'd never done before with prey.

He kissed him.

It was a tender kiss, his lips pressed softly against Casey's, his tongue softly entering his mouth. Completely the opposite of the face-fucking moments before, it was gentle rather than savage.

Suddenly the hunter pulled back.

What the fuck was he doing?

He had captured this guy in order to sell him and make a nice profit, and here he was kissing him like they were a goddamn couple.

Pull yourself together! Curtis angrily told himself.

He moved back and, grabbing Casey's legs, roughly flipped him over onto his stomach, the young man's head twisted on the pillow. Then he yanked down the boy's tight cutoff jeans, getting access to his butt.

Straddling his prey's body farther down this time, Curtis pulled Casey's asscheeks apart and buried his face between them. It was nice in there, soft yet firm, with the spectacular scent of the young man's masculinity seeping into his nose. The hunter tongued his prey's asshole, pushing his tongue into the tiny ring of muscle. Curtis tongue-fucked Casey for a while, enjoying the sensations, as his cock, getting harder and harder, desperately wanted to get inside, too.

Soon the hunter could no longer delay his pleasure, and he pulled himself up, away from the limp body on the bed. It was his dick's turn. A few squirts from a tube of lube and his cock was ready for action. Casey's asshole, already open and ready from the tongue-fucking, took Curtis's invasion without protest. Curtis closed his eyes and savored what was surely one of the finest pleasures a man could experience: the hunter fucking his prey. As he repeatedly thrust into the young man, he tried, despite the temptation to get lost in ecstasy, to stay alert for signs that Casey was waking up. Maybe he should have dosed him with more of the drug before entering him, but the temptation was too great: *he had to fuck him now.*

Still, his prey lay on the bed, motionless, inhaling the deep breaths of the unconscious. Curtis was confident he would be finished before Casey woke up.

As he moved his cock in and out of his prey, the hunter thought of the hunt. Of the young man looking at him hungrily, his eyes roving up and down his body, his smile, the experience of seeing Casey's eyelids flutter as the drug worked on him, the sensation of the young man collapsing in his arms, and the feeling of slinging him over his shoulder, picking him up and carrying him back to his lair, like a caveman with an animal he'd hunted down.

"You didn't have to knock me out, you know," Casey said.

Curtis froze in mid-fuck.

"What?" he said.

"I would've come with you wherever you wanted to take me. You didn't have to drug me. See, I came to the fair looking for a master."

"How long have you been awake?"

"A few minutes."

"How do you know who you're talking to?" Curtis asked, looking down at Casey's back. Although the young man's head was turned to the left, the angle was too severe: he couldn't see the face of the man whose cock was in his ass.

"I recognize your boots on the floor there," Casey said. Curtis followed with his eyes to where his boots, harness, and chaps lay in pile a few feet away from the bed, right in Casey's field of vision. "I noticed the slash on the left one when you walked back with the beers."

This was certainly a day of firsts.

The hunter had never had a capture wake up so quietly; usually they moaned and thrashed around as they rose out of unconsciousness, giving him plenty of time to finish his fucking and get ready with a new dose of the knockout drug.

Curtis knew he had to think fast.

"I thought you might need some persuasion," he said.

"To go with a guy as hot as you?" Casey said, "No way. I wanted to be your bottomboy as soon as I laid eyes on you."

The hunter felt something moving in his heart.

Damn it, this can't happen! A hunter can't fall for his prey. He has to remain apart from them, separate from them, objectify them. Capture, test, and sell.

"Don't let me stop you," Casey said.

"What?"

"Go ahead with what you were doing...."

The hunter realized that his hard cock was still in his prey's butt.

"Oh, yeah, okay..." he said. He was amazed that he was still stiff, what with the guy waking up and all. But it felt so good to be inside him, to be fucking him, that he'd almost been ready to shoot when Casey started talking.

What the hell, he thought, and resumed his fuck. *What the hell.*

Casey murmured submissively as he was raped by the hunter who had captured him. Curtis threw him as brutal a fuck as he'd ever given, and it was fucking awesome. The hunter knew he was pounding his prey's ass freaking hard, but Casey never complained, just moaned like the true bottomboy he was. As the hunter fucked him, he realized that he didn't want this to be the only time he did this. He knew the rules of the hunt, but he didn't think he could follow through this time.

"I'm gonna shoot, man!" Curtis growled.

"Yeah, fill me up, Sir, fill me with your hot cum, *please, Sir!*" Casey begged.

The hunter roared as he came inside his prey, his orgasm ripping through him as his cock shot spurt after spurt of spunk into the young man. When he was done, Curtis pulled out of Casey, unshackled his wrists and ankles, and collapsed on the bed next to him. His prey put his arms around him and rested his head on the hunter's chest. Curtis had half expected Casey to run as soon as he'd gotten off him, but he was doing exactly the opposite.

Prey held hunter as Curtis's body slowly recovered from the tremendous orgasm that had flowed through him. He'd never felt this way about prey before. It was scary.

And awesome.

They lay there for a while before either spoke again. Casey turned his head so he could look into Curtis's eyes.

"Sir?" he said.

"Yeah?"

"After you got me here and fucked me, what were you going to do with me?"

The hunter debated whether or not he should tell the truth. Honesty, after all, was very important when embarking on a new relationship.

"Well, Casey, I was going to sell you. But I changed my mind."

"And what did you decide?"

"That I'm keeping you."

"I was hoping you'd say that," Casey said, laying his head back on Curtis's chest, "Sir."

DADDY'S DESSERT

Doug Harrison

Brad slept until noon on Saturday. His desire to present a clean and tidy environment superseded his annoyance at housecleaning. "This boy needs a boy," he thought. He wore a tattered and soiled jock and a faded pink apron with *To Hell with Housework* stenciled in large black letters. He spun his apron front to rear whenever he plunked his sweaty bubble butt on a freshly dusted chair.

He washed the week's dishes, swept the floor, and shoved his empty TV dinner packages into the garbage. Next, he vacuumed the living room, grunting as he pushed and pulled the clunky cleaner, heavy with its overfull bag. He dusted end tables and coffee table, even lifting lamps and magazines. Finally, he polished his combat boots and leather jock. As an afterthought, he organized the whips, hoods, and harnesses tucked adjacent to his leather jackets in the rear of the long walk-in closet.

He douched, deftly shaved his relaxed balls, and douched

again. He reveled in the warm water filling his butthole. "I hope something else is rammed up here tonight," he leered. "Something big and hard, and propelled by two hundred pounds of strong, wild daddy." He stepped out of his lengthy shower into the steam-filled bathroom, wiped the mirror, and trimmed the unruly strands of chest hair that covered his large nipples. He grinned at his reflection.

The doorbell rang at 5:50. Brad adjusted his leather jock one last time and swung open the door. Erwin loomed two inches taller than Brad. He wore a leather cap, and his faded 501s, a size or two too small, drew attention to his substantial thighs and emphasized his bulging crotch. Two overstuffed shopping bags could not conceal the massive shoulders that stretched his leather vest.

He looked Brad up and down. "Nice. Going to let me in, boy? Doesn't matter, I've been invited." He pushed past Brad and marched through the living room. He stopped and scanned four large prints in gilded frames evenly spaced above the brown leather couch.

"Wagner's *Ring,*" he pronounced.

Brad nodded.

"Rackham," Erwin stated matter-of-factly.

"You're the only visitor who recognized the *Ring,* let alone the painter."

"I've seen the *Ring* in Munich."

"We have a lot to discuss."

"Perhaps."

Erwin continued into the kitchen and plopped his grocery bags onto the small counter. He sneered at the microwave.

"Where are the pots and pans?"

"In the oven," Brad cringed.

Erwin shook his head, and opened the oven door. "Should

have brought my own." He looked at Brad. "Get my backpack from the car."

"But, but…the neighbors."

"Don't argue with me, boy. Anyone who notices you should consider themselves lucky. Now go."

"Yes, Sir."

Brad paused behind an accommodating redwood adjacent to the front porch. He loved the trees on his property, sturdy sentinels from the primordial past. A collage of rustling needles scattered light across the veranda and onto Brad's naked torso. His neighbor, Martha, was watering her petunias. He jounced down the steps two at a time, sprinted to the rear door of Erwin's dirty blue Volvo, and yanked the handle.

Locked.

Brad peered down the driveway, took a deep breath, and stepped sideways around the car, careful that his ass didn't face the street. He opened the other rear door, retrieved the backpack, and raced up the steps.

"What took you so long?" Erwin looked out the window. Martha was watering her side yard, her head cocked toward Brad's front porch. "I see. Come here."

Brad approached and lowered his head.

"You're so endearing." Erwin grabbed Brad's almond-colored hair, jerked his head back, and covered his mouth with thick lips. He buried his tongue in Brad's throat. Brad moaned as his tongue danced around Erwin's. Erwin clamped Brad's nostrils shut and blew into his mouth. He ground his crotch into Brad's jock. Brad felt Erwin's hard-on despite the thick leather covering his own rigid cock. Dizziness grabbed Brad. His eyes bulged and his body shuddered.

Erwin held Brad under his armpits. "Okay?"

Stale air exploded from Brad's lungs. He gulped and nodded.

"Good. Now, pick roses for a centerpiece, and be quick about it." Erwin strode to the sink, and added over his shoulder, "Regardless of who's out there."

"Yes, Sir." Brad exited into the side yard. He retrieved heavy gloves, clippers, and a large orange pail from the storeroom under the front porch, and jogged down the sloping lawn.

His rose garden. His pride and joy. Over thirty bushes. Brad made his way to the tall Chrysler Imperials. He was always drawn to their deep red hue, his favorite color. Though he twisted and turned, low thorns grabbed his ass and legs. "Too bad they aren't scratching my nipples," he thought. He cut several burgundy beauties and added a few long-stemmed Black Magics. He leaned against a redwood, one hip thrust forward like a whore boy claiming a lucrative lamppost, and admired the collage in his bucket. He wiggled his butt as he adjusted his jock, glanced at the house, winced, and rushed up the stairs.

A brown leather armchair had found its way from his office to the center of the kitchen. Erwin's backpack leaned against a rear leg. He inspected Brad's offering and nodded.

"Good job." He had changed into a black leather jock that complemented his vest. The laces of his knee-high black leather boots stretched over thick calves. Brad gasped at the perfectly well-rounded, firm ass. He wanted to bury his face between those cheeks. Erwin's thigh muscles rippled as he crossed the kitchen, marched to the armchair with military precision, and sat. He looked at Brad.

Brad approached. Erwin grabbed Brad's jock in midstride, unsnapped it, and flung it to the side. A quick smile escaped his lips at the sound of the jock's thunk, and the sight of Brad's boner.

"Kneel."

Brad dropped, head bowed, hands behind his back. Erwin held a narrow black leather collar under Brad's nose and Brad inhaled deeply to savor the pungent aroma. Erwin wrapped the collar around Brad's neck, paused, and cinched it. He dangled a small black lock in front of Brad's face and gave it a quick kiss. Brad closed his eyes. Erwin snapped the lock shut. "Such a nice sound," he whispered.

"Thank you, Daddy." Brad wrapped his arms around Erwin's waist, and buried his head in his lap.

"You like this, don't you boy?"

Brad looked up through cloudy eyes. "Yes, Sir," he sighed, "more than you'll ever know."

"I do know, I've been there," Erwin countered. "Tell me why you like it."

Brad bit his lower lip. "Because I'm yours, even for a short time. I can give it all up. I don't have to make any decisions. I can just be. Be...yours."

"You like not running the show?"

"Yes, Sir."

"So don't try, not even a little bit. Understand?"

"Yes, Sir."

"Good boy. Sit down."

Brad took Erwin's place in the chair. He rolled his back to contact the maximum amount of stiff leather, pressed his arms into the armrests, and spread his calves against the wooden legs. He gripped the knurled palm rests, exhaled, and settled into his self-imposed bondage.

Erwin nodded and lifted two coils of nylon rope, flat, and three quarters of an inch wide. "These are used to lash cargo pallets. You'll like the feel of them. The colors match the roses you picked."

Brad smiled.

Erwin cocked his head. "Hmmm, tell me boy, what's so special with red and black?"

"Red has been my favorite color since I was a kid. I don't know why." His face wrinkled in concentration. "Even before puberty, red signified passion. Fiery but touchable, perhaps obtainable." He paused. "An archetypical memory of the collective unconscious."

"Don't get too heavy, boy."

Brad swallowed his disappointment. They wouldn't be discussing the final scene of *The Ring* before drifting off to sleep in each other's arms. "Black is absence of color; it's quiet and peaceful, like when I trance out in a heavy scene."

"Anything else?"

"I had the handles of my floggers braided with intertwined black and red leather."

"Are you any good?"

"Uh...several tops...ah...both male and female, have asked me to flog them."

Erwin raised his eyebrows. "So my boy wears several hats?"

"As they fit, Sir." Brad emphasized the last word.

Erwin stepped behind Brad. "Maybe sometime I'll order you to flog me," he said as he pulled a six-foot length of red strap across Brad's chest and slid a section back and forth over his perky nipples with taut, short strokes. He smirked as Brad moaned, arranged the strip symmetrically under Brad's armpits, and secured it with a tight double knot. He crisscrossed the remainder over Brad's chest and tied each end to the backrest, such that Brad's nipples were not only accessible, but also precisely framed.

"Can you breathe?"

"Yes, Sir," Brad moaned.

Erwin ran red bands over Brad's thighs from waist to knees, and knotted them under the seat. He tied Brad's arms with red straps, and his calves with black straps. He stood back and nodded. Brad slid into sensuous submission marked by shallow breathing and an unblinking stare.

"You're a pretty sight, boy. Very nice tits. Huge." Erwin knelt and flicked his tongue over each nipple. He chewed and bit, then stood and grabbed both, digging his fingers in and pulling. Brad shrieked and tried to stomp his feet.

"Shit, you're so much fun, boy." Erwin yanked upward, and Brad pushed down into his boots.

"Fuck, fuck, fuck, Sir," he screamed. Erwin tugged, and the chair hopscotched inch by inch toward the sink. Brad wailed and growled. Erwin gave a last yank and wiped Brad's face with a damp paper towel. He passed a steady stream of cold water to Brad, mouth to mouth. He waited, hands on hips, until Brad stopped gulping and then he unsnapped the leather pouch of his own jock. His thick, uncut dick jumped out and he pulled back the foreskin. The end glistened with precum. Brad strained to move his head closer.

"Every bit as big as you expected?" Without waiting for a reply, Erwin straddled the chair, clutched his cock, and slid the tip across Brad's mouth. Brad licked his lips and stretched his jaws like a baby bird straining for its worm. Erwin stepped back.

"Now for the appetizer and the main course. But first your roses." He grabbed a pair of scissors from the knife rack, and swiftly but precisely made an attractive arrangement. He saved two buds, red and black, and trimmed their stems. He forced them between the straps crossing Brad's upper chest, so that thorns dug into Brad's nipples and buds tickled his chin. Brad squirmed but remained silent as drops of blood congealed under each nipple.

Erwin slid a long knife from his backpack and smacked the flat of the blade against his open palm. "This is what a chef's knife looks like, boy." He skimmed the tip across Brad's dry lower lip, exploring each crease and teasing a whisker or two, conjuring beads of perspiration. He slid the knife-edge down along Brad's cheek and drew it across his motionless Adam's apple. Erwin stood back until Brad's frozen body relaxed enough to quiver.

He moved with authority about the kitchen, food flying from counter to cutting board. His knife rose and fell in quick, steady motions. *Chop. Chop. Chop.* Erwin scraped perfectly diced avocado, onion, and tomato cubes into a bowl with a conductor's flourish, added lemon juice, olive oil, and Tabasco sauce as if executing a drumroll, and finished with syncopated dashes of salt and pepper. He used a large wooden spoon to deftly transform the ingredients into a smooth mixture; Brad wondered how many boys had smarted from the spoon's sting.

Erwin plunged his middle finger into the dressing and turned to Brad, whose mouth reacted with a perfect O. Erwin shoved his guacamole-coated digit in with a quick jab. Brad licked it clean during Erwin's finger-fucking motions. Erwin ambled to the counter and fiddled for a few moments, his hands at his crotch. He sidled toward Brad. His dick continued to jut forward in majestic profile, but one hand covered the end.

"Okay, boy, here's your first course." Two fingers pinched the end of his foreskin, which bulged like the bowl of a speed pipe. "Open up, boy."

Brad spread his jaws as ordered.

"Lick me clean, boy."

Brad's mouth strained to contain the mixture of cock and guacamole. He worked his jaw muscles to swallow the dip as it oozed from Erwin's stuffed foreskin. Erwin pushed the back of

Brad's head with a firm one-handed grasp, and rubbed his shoulders with the other. Brad's well-trained throat muscles guided the guacamole downward, like an anaconda ingesting its prey, until he could loosen his lips and lick Erwin's dickhead clean. He tasted precum, and nodded.

"Enjoy it, boy?"

"Wow! Yes, Sir, thank you, Sir."

"So did I, boy. No one's cleaned me off this good before." He swatted Brad's cock, causing it to rock back and forth in syncopation to his own. "Have any cock cages around here?"

Brad nodded. "In the center bureau drawer in the bedroom." Erwin marched off. Brad tightened his ass muscles and strained to thrust. He relaxed and eavesdropped on the humming and rummaging sounds tumbling through the house.

Erwin returned with a leather and metal contraption, replete with lock and key. "I've never seen one with this many rings," he said.

"It's custom made. I had an extra ring added."

"I'll have fun putting this on you." Erwin held the cage up by one strap and admired it. It contained four metal rings, spaced apart by three riveted straps that secured a metal cage at the end. An engorged cockhead would be accessible to admirers and tormenters. The device was held in place by an adjustable, lockable leather strap.

It was obvious that Brad's rigid cock could not be crammed into the enclosure.

"Have any rubber bands, boy?"

"Hanging from the doorknob, Sir."

"Of course."

Erwin moved a paper-thin slice of pale processed turkey meat from the main compartment of the refrigerator to the freezer. After a few moments, he secured it around Brad's dick with rubber bands. Brad shrieked and shivered as his dick shriveled. Erwin covered the turkey with lube, maneuvered the cock cage into place, and secured the leather strap with a small padlock. Brad's dick reached half the length of the cage.

"You'll grow into it as your meat warms up," Erwin chuckled, and removed rubber bands and turkey. To Brad's surprise and disappointment, Erwin held out a bottle of mineral water, rather than pissing in his mouth.

"I'm going to untie you now. Set the table with one setting of china and the sterling silverware that I noticed in the closet, and I'll finish cooking."

"Yes, Sir." Straps flew in all directions and landed on the floor in a tangled maze. Brad resisted the temptation to coil them, and meandered through the succulent odors emanating from the stove into the dining room. He stood motionless a few seconds, touched his collar, and caressed his cock cage.

He placed the china delicately on the table, fussed with its exact location, and stood back before folding a white cloth napkin on the right side of the dinner plate, moving it to the left, and arranging the silver. He'd rather have been licking dirty boots. He walked back to the kitchen.

"Perfect timing. I'm finished here." Erwin shut off the burners and retrieved a dinner plate from the dining room. "You set an elegant table, boy."

Brad stood motionless, hands behind his back.

Erin removed a large black plastic doggie bowl from his bag, arranged chicken fajitas on his plate, then dumped a similar meal into Brad's bowl. He placed his own meal on the table, Brad's under it, and secured Brad with a leather leash that stretched from collar to table leg.

"Go for it, puppy boy," he ordered. "It's okay to use your hands."

Brad busied himself with a few perfunctory bites while Erwin cleaned his plate.

Erwin leaned back in his chair, balancing on the two rear legs. He removed food particles from his teeth and gums with the tip of his tongue, chomped on a blue pill, and swallowed the concoction with a water chaser. His left hand flopped down and rested on Brad's shoulder. Brad shuddered. Erwin smirked. "Relax, boy, relax," he said. "I won't hurt you"—he opened his mouth like a freshly carved jack-o'-lantern, and ran his tongue around his lips—"much." He smacked Brad on the ass. "Get up, puppy."

"Yes, Sir." Brad's head grazed the table edge, he ducked, and his backside pointed upward toward the painting of Siegfried brandishing his sword.

"You mentioned you have a collection of leather hoods. Where are they?"

"On the top rear shelf in the hall closet, Sir."

Erwin nodded and disappeared. His humming played counterpoint with the swishing sound of leather on leather as he shuffled the deck of hoods.

Then silence. Thoughtful silence. Menacing silence.

Erwin strode into view with the hood of hoods, all black leather. A soft inner lining zipped shut from top of head to nape of neck. A thick outer layer laced shut with a leather thong that crisscrossed its way through shiny metal nubbins and ended in a tight *X* formed by four hitching posts and secured by a knot or bow, Top's choice. Erwin held it on his fist; it covered most of his forearm. It lacked eye and mouth openings. Two small grommets rested at the base of the carefully crafted nose. He pushed it into Brad's face.

"Like the smell, boy?"

Brad trembled. His fear hung between the two men like a motionless cloud between two mountain peaks.

"A little scared, are we, boy?"

Brad's jaw dropped.

"Answer me, boy!"

"Yes, Sir, I'm scared."

Erwin rested his free hand on Brad's chest, and lowered the hood onto the hefty arm of the couch. He reverently smoothed the hood's contours as if coaxing Brad's panting to slow. With a magician's deft hands, he pulled a rectangular mirror, a one-edged razor blade, and a small plastic bag containing irregular chunks of white powder from a zipped pocket of his backpack.

"I brought a little bit of Tina, just in case. You're special. Let's go there."

Brad backed up a step. "Do you want me or the drug?"

"Both. Lighten up. It's just a little."

"It sounded like you were in recovery."

"Some days I'm in recovery, some days I'm not," Erwin shot back. "Relax." Brad sunk into the couch and folded his arms across his chest.

Erwin cut one chunk of meth into fine particulates with dexterous, crosshatched motions. *Chop. Chop. Chop.* He separated the fine powder into four lines that beckoned from the smooth, shiny surface of the mirror. He slid two lines into a grungy glass pipe and lit the powder with a crème brûlée torch. He drew on the pipe and exhaled a thin pillar of smoke.

"Good stuff," he said. He ogled Brad. "Kneel with your chest on the couch and spread your asscheeks." Brad complied. Erwin's index finger, wet with spit, explored the folds of Brad's sphincter. He slid his finger in and Brad's hole opened. "Good boy. This ain't no beginner's hole."

Erwin took another drag, closed his mouth over Brad's asshole, and leisurely exhaled. Brad felt smoke wend its way into his innards.

"Feeling okay, boy?"

Brad's body tingled as a warm glow raced from pore to pore. "More than okay, Sir. Thank you, Sir."

Erwin reached under Brad's chest and brushed his nipples. Brad's dick hardened with short jerks as it filled the cock cage.

"Oh, damn, Sir, you make me feel sooo good. Thank you so much, Sir." His body shook.

"Sit up, boy, and relax."

Brad righted himself, fought off the urge to hop to his feet, and grasped his knees to still his fidgety legs and arms. His cockhead thumped against the metal end of the cage. He bit his tongue. But his eyes held steady on Erwin, who jumped up and strode to the table. He inhaled one line, splitting it between each nostril. His nose wiggled and wrinkled as he tossed his head back and sniffed. He looked at Brad with sparkling eyes, lurched, grabbed Brad, and shoved his tongue into Brad's mouth. He fucked Brad's trembling lips, and stuck his tongue deep into Brad's throat. Brad's tongue peeked out and its tip wavered on Erwin's lips. "That's it, boy, give it back to Daddy," Erwin ordered. Brad complied, and two tongues fought for possession of the other's mouth with dancing, lunging passion, like snakes exploring a den and struggling to mate.

Erwin drew back, took a deep breath, and exhaled, a soft sound, like a gentle breeze finding its way through high redwood boughs. "Nice mouth, boy," he murmured.

"Thank you, Sir."

Erwin drew back his foreskin. He had dusted his cockhead with white powder. "Worship my dick, boy."

Brad smiled.

"This is what you've been waiting for, isn't it, boy?"

"Uh, yes, Sir."

Erwin sprawled on the couch, spread his legs, threw his

head back, and closed his eyes. Brad knelt, pulled back Erwin's foreskin, and cocked his head like a curious puppy as he stared at the speckled cockhead. He pursed his lips gingerly around it, and slid the head slowly over his moist lips, along his furrowed tongue, and with increased gusto across the roof of his mouth.

Brad puckered his cheeks to gather saliva that he swished over Erwin's dickhead. He swallowed his spit with a loud gulp. Erwin grabbed Brad's head and jammed his cock in with a lunge of his hips. Brad gagged. Erwin pumped. Brad gagged again. Erwin withdrew, and sunk back into the couch. "You're learning, boy. It'll take time, but I'll train you," he said while Brad retched on all fours. Finally, Brad sat back on his haunches and looked at Erwin through tear-clogged eyes.

Erwin gave Brad a glass of water. Brad gulped half and Erwin drained the remainder.

"Ready for the hood, boy?"

"Uh...I suppose so."

Brad watched as Erwin tightened a pair of kneepads into place. He offered none to Brad, though several were stacked on the closet shelf. The two men faced each other. Erwin dangled the hood between them. Brad gulped air like a medieval prisoner about to be buried alive, savoring his last full inhalations. Erwin pulled the hood over Brad's head and zipped the inner lining shut with a fluid motion. He jiggled the hood until the nose grommets lay under Brad's nostrils. Erwin laced the outer leather skin closed by threading a leather thong between the two rows of nubbins on both sides of the hood. He yanked, pulled and tightened the thong until there was no slack. None.

"Still okay, boy?" he shouted.

Brad nodded.

"On your knees!"

Erwin rolled on a condom, then knelt behind Brad and smeared his asshole with a mixture of speed and lube. Then he grabbed Brad's hips and plunged in.

Brad jumped at the initial assault. Erwin ground his fingers into Brad's hips. He thrust, pushed, and rammed his dick. When he was all the way in, he paused.

He lowered his torso onto Brad's back.

"It's all right, boy, we're there."

Brad didn't know what ached more, his asshole or his skinned knees from hopscotching across the rug. He waited for Erwin to continue his fucking.

Which he did.

Two hundred pounds of daddy propelled Brad's head into the wall.

"Shit," Erwin yelled. "You all right, boy?"

Brad nodded. Padding was the saving grace of the hood.

Erwin continued his mission for some time; it was, in fact, a good fuck. But his performance slid from enthusiastic to mechanical as total release proved elusive. He withdrew his flaccid cock, yanked off the rubber, and threw it into the fireplace. Brad didn't move.

Erwin guided Brad to a standing position. He loosened the hood, yanked it off, and pitched it onto the couch. Brad squinted into the bright light.

"That was great, Daddy. Thank you."

"Kneel," Erwin commanded. "Open your mouth."

Brad looked up as Erwin placed his cock in Brad's mouth.

"This is something else you've wanted, isn't it, boy?" The first few drops of piss crossed Brad's tongue. "There's a lot," Erwin stated as the flow increased.

Brad was no novice. He swallowed with his mouth open, and kept pace with the torrent. He reveled in its pungent odor and bitter taste. Best of all, he liked receiving a gift from Daddy, of Daddy. Just as he wondered how much more his distended stomach could take, Erwin's stream diminished to surges, then a trickle, then stopped. Erwin shook the few remaining drops across Brad's face.

"Thank you, Daddy," Brad said.

"Welcome, boy. You'll get a buzz from this. Something to remember me by."

"Huh?"

"I have to leave. Now."

"You're not staying the night?"

"My mother gets upset if I come home after the sun comes up. If I'm gone for more than a day, she looks for track marks on my arm."

Erwin changed into his original outfit and scurried about the house scooping his few belongings into his backpack. He smoothed the wrinkles in his 501s and pecked Brad on the cheek. "Good time, boy. I'll give you a call." He disappeared through the front doorway into the shadows on the porch.

Brad stood in the hallway. The rapid clumping of Erwin's boots punctuated Brad's shivers and belches. He darted into the bedroom, yanked on a dresser drawer, and pulled out a butt plug. He heard Erwin clamor down the front steps. Brad pushed the butt plug into his well-lubed asshole and clenched. A rubber puppy tail curled out and up from his butt and wiggled with his slightest movement. He ran outside and paused at the top of the steps. Erwin had backed his car to the end of the driveway. He started down the hill without waving.

Martha's kitchen lights blazed forth. Brad jumped. Shit! The metal on his cock cage sparkled. He charged into the house, slammed the front door, and leaned back into it. He dug his heels into the rug and scanned the mess.

To clean, to play, or perchance to dream. Not a difficult choice.

Brad tore open the plastic bag and licked the few remaining grains of powder. He scampered into the bedroom, grabbed his favorite nipple clamps, and tightened them with quick jerks. He grimaced at the familiar sharp pains that retreated into time-honored dull throbs. He grabbed his pink apron and hurried toward the kitchen.

REFUGEES

Elazarus Wills

It was the sign that caught Stern's eye. *Good's Leather.* To find those two familiar words in the middle of the Kansas prairie was like seeing a wheat grower's co-op spring up on West Colfax next to a strip club. Stern had left the interstate a couple of hundred miles into Kansas, to score gas and enough Diet Pepsi to get him through to Missouri or Iowa. He had filled up the vintage MG Midget in Denver before leaving, but now the needle was a fly's ass below the quarter mark, and the cooler on the floor of the passenger side was filled with tepid water, floating Snickers bar wrappers, and sunken recyclable aluminum.

Food/Gas/Lodging next right. Up the ramp and into the Esso station, except there was no Esso station. Just a thirty-foot-high sign he had seen from the highway and the roofless, burned-out shell of a convenience store. *Fuck.* South of the ramp, maybe a half mile, Stern could make out the remains of some long-ago bypassed little farm town, probably setting its sails to blow away as soon as the last of the groundwater was sucked out of the dwindling aquifer, swallowed and pissed back out by the thousands of factory-farm hogs. He had seen the rows of low metal buildings squatting on the sunburned prairie a few miles back. A happening place.

It was nothing new to Stern. He had been born in Kansas, in a similar place eighty or so miles west of Hutchinson. He had less than no desire to revisit his past or anything resembling it, and he was now regretting not taking the northern route through Nebraska. The scenery there wasn't much different, but it did have the recommendation of not being his home state. He needed gas. He drove on into town. *Tice, Kansas: Population 872.* It was an old sign, wooden, peeling, and leaning slightly toward the north. Someone had spray painted a lopsided pair of red lips at the bottom. The paint of the graffiti was peeling too. He stopped and took a picture of the sign with his digital camera. Heartland kitsch.

The buildings in the block-long downtown business district were largely unoccupied. Asphalt-roofed, false-fronted buildings of a story and a half or two predominated. Stern thought he saw something at the end of the block that looked like a gas pump. Probably a farmer's co-op or something. There were three pickups and one dusty car parked in the whole block. Then he saw the sign. *Good's Leather.* Painted in red lettering with black outlines on the glass of a storefront. There was an old saddle on a sawhorse out front. An American flag was mounted on a bracket over the door. Stern pulled the little car to the curb. *Why not?*

A cowbell attached to the door clanged as Stern entered. The smell of the place was wonderful. Leather everywhere. Dozens of saddles were displayed in the large room, some old, some looking brand new. All typically western in design, with potent masculine pommels, fancy leather carving, and silver details.

Dividing the room was a waist-high counter, in the middle of which stood a snarling wolf. A taxidermist's glass-eyed full-body mount. One half of the store was a showroom for the saddles and the other looked to be a workshop. A mounted bison head hung on one wall above a display of its wooly hide. A radio was on in the corner playing what passed for modern country music, 70s white-bread rock with steel guitar breaks thrown in. Stern had moved over to the counter when the cowbell clanged behind him. He turned to see a tall, familiar-looking man, wearing a blue-and-white-striped cloth railroader's hat, holding a large white ceramic cup in one hand.

"Sorry. I was getting some coffee next door. I never bother to lock the door around here," the newcomer said. His eyes showed surprise. "Wait...I think I know you. Back in the day. Stern something—from Denver, right?" The man was black, but not *black-black;* cocoa skin the color of stained leather. Caribbean sexy. Full, sensuous lips and wide brown eyes.

Stern stared at him. "Noah! What the fuck? You died in nineteen-ninety!"

"I moved," Noah said. "Who said I died?"

"Well, everyone knew you were sick. And then you were suddenly not there and I heard you had gone home to Michigan...." Fifteen years before, Noah had seemed just another typical story of the unlucky or foolish in the insular Denver gay scene. The ones who stuck around got the obligatory visits from friends while in the hospital, and between those, at home. Eventually, the well-attended funeral. The others, and Stern remembered a lot of them, had just packed up and left, to be buried quietly, like other familial embarrassments, by relatives who had been proven right. *A bad end.*

"To die? I guess I can understand the circumstantial evidence. I thought so myself at the time," Noah said. "But I only made it as far as Kansas. Now I seem to be fine, am fine, or at least in a holding pattern." He looked healthy to Stern, tall, strong, and rugged. A full six inches taller than the compact Stern, he looked better now as an older man than he had a decade and a half before. *Noah Good.*

"So now you make—saddles?" Stern asked. He took in a deep breath. God, he loved the smell of leather.

Noah moved over behind his counter. "Saddles, saddlebags, bridles, and all kinds of fancy tack. I have a friend here who's a metalsmith. He does the silver conchos and the bits. Handmade buckles for my carved belts." He must have seen something in Stern's face. "Straight friend. Pretty straight town too."

"Straight state," Stern said. "I'm on my way to Boston. Ghostwriting job doing a memoir for an ex-politician. Famous homophobe, who now that he's seventy-something, wants to come out—and make amends."

"Better late, but good for you. And the novels?"

"Not ready for prime time. Other stuff pays a lot better."

"I still make a few of the harnesses and collars. A few other things," Noah said. "The Internet has really changed the leather goods market. Let me show you." He motioned Stern back behind the counter.

Elaborate body harnesses like the ones Noah had been famous for in Denver. Even better than those. *Good's Leather.* Leather hoods and masks.

"Whoa...." Stern had said when he saw the second small display room. "So you haven't gone totally native?"

"Well, I have changed a lot." Noah sat down in a chair. A black, leather-upholstered chair, Stern noted. "From this distance, the role-playing and rules seem a little silly. I don't think I could manage it now without heavy irony."

"Not to mention that properly trainable houseboys are hard to come by in these modern times," Stern said, admiring a hand-tooled, silver-accented harness that looked like it could have belonged to Conan the Barbarian. All that was absent was a huge sword and a scabbard on the belt. He couldn't recall Noah as being a master *or* submissive, just the ultimate model for displaying his leather-craftsman skills. Making an appearance at the right party or theme night. They had been casual friends, never lovers, leather or otherwise. "So...do you like it out here? I mean compared to the city...."

"This is where I am going to die," Noah said softly, then, seeing a look on Stern's face. "When I'm eighty-five, hopefully, not next week. It's just that I'm home here. I'm done. Nail my shoes to the kitchen floor and all of that. Hard to believe right? From a city boy raised in L.A.?"

"Wow." Stern thought about growing up in Kansas and never feeling at home. An alien in a land that had it in for aliens. "Aren't you lonely out here? I mean, don't you just have to get in the car and head for the city for a weekend once in a while?" *Sixteen and standing by the side of the highway with a gym bag and his thumb out.*

"No, I never have," Noah said. "I've been tempted, but with everything—I just mostly stay home. Plus, I like an ordered life."

"An ordered life," Stern echoed. "There is that. I have a pretty ordered life, too." He stared at Noah in his leather chair and met his eyes. *Those eyes.* He and Noah smiled at the same moment.

"Could you kiss me?" Noah asked as he stood up. "It's been a while—a very long while. Like I said—a holding pattern. Maybe my lips don't work anymore."

Stern recovered from his initial shock, laughed, and stepped into the taller man's embrace. The kiss began with lips barely touching. Feather soft, caressing lips. Exploring lips. Lips reaching into the unknown. Stern could feel Noah's breath intermingling with his own. Stern kept his eyes open and heard the equally wide-eyed Noah make a rumbling giggle of a sound. Stern wondered if what he was feeling was being communicated in *his* eyes. He wasn't sure what was in Noah's eyes, but it wasn't discouragement.

"Your lips still work," Stern whispered. "You never kissed me—before. Back then."

A long pause, lips parted and tongues extending—serpent-like. "I remember wanting to, but with you leather guys it was a power thing. Everyone in his place."

"I'm not a leatherman anymore, not that I seriously was, ever. Not really," Stern said as he allowed Noah to unbutton his shirt. "Not for ten years."

"So we're a couple of backsliding heretics," Noah's teeth were on his nipples.

"Who were just poseurs at the time. But you still make the leather, and I still get a hard-on when I see a guy in a leather vest." Stern reached down and popped a row of the snaps on Noah's western-style shirt. He was greeted by thick, curly chest hair. "You don't wax anymore." Memories of dim lights playing on smooth, oiled chests restrained with leather straps.

"Neither do you."

Stern felt Noah undo his khakis, a hand sliding into his briefs, squeezing and stroking. Then the trousers and underwear were swept downward and Noah straightened. Stern gasped at the feel of Noah's work-roughened hands clasping his buttocks with power and authority. No hesitation. No permission asked. Working by touch, since their mouths were now hard against each other, Stern undid Noah's heavy belt and lowered the zipper on the snug blue jeans.

Noah placed a palm on Stern's chest and moved him outward to an arm's length. Then, with a smile, he slipped his own pants down and off and stood naked. Stern made to remove his own trousers, which hung about his knees.

"No." Noah's command was soft and low, but definitely a command.

"No?"

"No." Noah's hands once again captured the cheeks of his ass and pulled Stern hard against him. "I want you to feel a little—restrained. A little off balance. Limited." The hands squeezed hard and then moved. Noah's cock pressed into Stern's stomach. "Sit down." Stern let himself be pushed into Noah's chair. The feel and cool texture of it against his naked back, thighs, and ass made him exhale with pleasure.

"This is starting to seem—familiar," Stern said.

"I have other, more familiar, things." Above him, Noah's grin was broad, sexy, and irresistible. He leaned down and took Stern's hard cock into his mouth, sliding down to the root, then back up and off. "Toys. Implements."

"Oh-my-god," Stern said, as saliva began to evaporate. He watched Noah open a drawer and extract leather straps about two inches wide and six feet long.

"Locally produced cowhide. Close to the source here," Noah said. He jerked a pair of the straps taut between his hands, producing a loud crack. "May I? Like I said, it's been a while." Stern could hear him breathe.

"Sure." He said it before he had fully processed what he was allowing. Noah picked up one of his wrists, making three quick turns with the leather and then running it through a steel buckle; three more turns around the oak arm of the chair, another buckle secured. Stern's right arm was held firmly to the chair. Then the left. He looked up into Noah's eyes. They gleamed with desire.

"One more thing," Noah said. "Just for the moment. Temporary." He held up a third piece of leather, elaborately stamped with a basket weave design. Silver buckle and a trio of riveted eagle medallions. "Please?"

Rational thoughts emerged in Stern's mind but he ignored them and nodded—then swallowed hard as the collar encircled his throat and was buckled in place.

A hand grasped Stern's organ at the root. He started to close his eyes with the pleasure of it all.

"Don't," Noah hissed, lips to lips. "Keep looking into my eyes. Don't close them. Don't look away. Don't..."

It wasn't an easy thing for Stern. Kissing, his own hands held immobile, other hands caressing, stroking, and pumping. Straining against the leather. Eyes locked onto the eyes of this man. The *leathermaker.* That was, he suddenly remembered, what they had called him. *Leathermaker.* Watching every nuance of building passion and desire and his own reactions reflected back to him in the one place where it was possible to see all of that. The eyes. Bared teeth and tightly stretched lips. The effort and eroticism of the watching. When he came, he saw it in Noah's eyes. Pleasure? Pride?

Noah was loosening the buckle on the right wrist and Stern allowed his hand to be turned wrist up, the strap retightened. Then the warm length of Noah's cock was in his palm. His fingers closed around it. It was wet and slippery as Noah's hips began to move. Stern had never stopped swimming in those brown eyes. They ached, pleaded, and finally they screamed. An instant later, Stern felt cum dripping over his clenched fingers.

"Welcome home to Kansas," Stern whispered, maybe to Noah but also to himself.

"Do you have to be back on the road today? Hang out here for a day and enjoy the slow life a little." Noah kissed his stomach, just below his navel.

Stern looked down at him, breathing hard with his mouth open trying to restrain the words. He managed only two. "Until tomorrow," he said.

Noah kissed him again, tongue entering his navel. "Let me take you to an early dinner," he suggested.

"Okay." Stern realized that he was very hungry. "You ever get to do this with one of the local cowboys?" He laughed at the look on Noah's face. They took turns in the bathroom, Stern first. He waited for Noah in the saddle showroom. The open sign was still up and the door unlocked. On the street outside, a blue pickup driven by a high-school-aged girl passed by.

The diner, two doors from the shop, on the other side of a dusty, unprosperous-looking thrift shop, was utilitarian. The Tice Café boasted a decor of 1970s-era vinyl, steel, and aluminum. Poorly matted and framed prints of Charles Russell paintings lined the white plaster walls. The menu was not printed, but rather, posted like in a fast-food restaurant on a large letter board in the back of the room, mounted over the serving window from the kitchen. Stern was shocked for a moment at how low the prices seemed. *Chicken Fried Steak - Dinner - $6.95. For Lunch or Breakfast - $4.95.*

The restaurant wasn't busy at four o'clock in the afternoon. An ancient man with thick plastic-framed glasses sat in a booth alone with a cup of coffee and an empty plate. A couple, also older, occupied the window booth and had watched them openly as they came in.

"Evening, Noah. How's business?" the man with the woman inquired. Noah said that business was fine and wasn't it a nice day? The woman smiled and greeted him. It seemed a rehearsed ritual to Stern. But pleasant, with more inner meaning than the actual words—like the Catholic Church of his childhood. Noah introduced him as a friend from Denver and led him to a booth all the way in the back. The old man sitting by himself hadn't acknowledged their presence at all.

"Well, welcome to Tice, what there is of it," the woman had said. "We don't get many visitors."

Stern figured that if this place was like his hometown, the usual Tice Café patrons were farm families who didn't come in until five or so. The waitress, who called Noah "Mr. Good," was a fleshy young woman in her midtwenties with huge breasts and a prominent wedding ring set. Stern ordered a chef salad and iced tea, while Noah had a sirloin with a baked potato. The salad came with strips of American cheese crisscrossed on top of iceberg lettuce, cubes of ham loaf, sliced tomatoes, and hard-boiled egg.

"That's the way they do it here," Noah said. "Cheddar, romaine, and Canadian bacon are for uppity fags from Kansas City."

"When in Rome..." Stern said, speared a pink chunk of processed ham on his fork, and deliberately chewed it. It tasted surprisingly pleasant, but then, he was very hungry. After a while the waitress refilled his plastic glass with more iced tea. They watched one another eat.

"I'm taking you home," Noah said as, steak eaten, he drank his black coffee.

"You can do that," Stern said.

"We can walk or you can drive me," Noah said. "I don't drive much. Just when I need to haul something. It's less than a mile." *Home.*

The house was a Midwestern saltbox farmhouse, blue with peach trim. A simple two-story rectangle with a steep, standing-seamed metal roof, and a lower addition and open porch on one side. A 60s vintage Ford pickup was parked in front of the good-sized barn. Stern parked the MG beside it. The view past the house was of gently undulating patchy-looking prairie to the horizon. A few black cattle wandered in the middle distance.

"National grasslands," Noah said. "Not much actual grass, but a lot of land. Old homesteads. Government got the land during the Depression dustbowl. Just leased for grazing now. Water'll be gone in forty years or less. After that, most of the people will have to move off."

"Then what will you do?" Stern asked.

"I'll be over eighty. I'll either be dead or paying someone to truck my drinking water from some other place with a river and a water treatment plant, or a way deeper well. I'm fucking glad I'm not one of those farmers."

It was the hour before sunset, when even the prairie, flat, brown, and uninspiring in the glare of midday, glowed like an Andrew Wyeth painting.

They kissed on the porch. Stern's hand went to Noah's crotch. "Careful," the leatherworker said.

"I think I've been *too* careful these last few years," Stern said.

"Careful is good," Noah said. "Sit down. Take a deep breath and listen to the crickets." He guided Stern to one of the wicker chairs. "I'll go get some wine." Stern leaned back and listened. There weren't any crickets but there *were* sounds. The distant barking of dogs and lowing of cattle. A barely there sound made by a rising and falling breeze moving through the grass. Noah came back with two glasses of wine, handed him one, and sat down.

"What do you think?" he asked.

Stern told him about growing up in Mazurton, not much bigger than this. Five or six hundred more people. "It seemed like a town where no one would choose to live. If you had prospects or dreams, you left. If you didn't, or were willing to live a limited life, you stayed. I knew how Sinclair Lewis felt."

"I couldn't have imagined this place before I came," Noah said. "I left Denver and was just driving east, thinking about maybe New York or Florida, but undecided. I was probably running on some buried belief that if I got really far away from where I got the virus I wouldn't have it anymore. Or maybe I would walk into the ocean and keep going. I stopped for lunch in Tice and some farmers were there, talking about how they had just plowed their wheat back into the ground because it hadn't rained enough that year. Everyone's concerns here were just so *different.*"

"So you decided to make a major lifestyle change. Live the good, square American heartland dream?" Stern sipped his wine.

"Well, it wasn't quite that quick," Noah said. "First I decided to hang around for a few days. I was exhausted. I rented a room and thought that I would spend a week breathing clean air—having no pressure. Watching people live real lives for a change. I though it would be good for me."

"Was it?"

"It seemed to work. By the end of the week I felt great. My energy was back. So I stayed another week and I even got my equipment out and started working." Noah stepped off the porch and tipped his face up to the sky, which had turned an evening shade of cobalt blue. "The guy I was sharing a house with worked on a ranch and asked if I could repair saddles. It wasn't that hard, and people appreciated what I did. A month after that I had the first shop opened, mostly doing tack repairs. I felt wonderful."

Stern had a sudden thought. "What are you taking?"

"Nothing."

"Nothing? But you can't..."

"I haven't taken anything stronger than Alka-Seltzer Plus since about six months after I got here," Noah said. "It got so I could even forget about the bug for weeks at a time. After about a year, I had the clinic here do a blood draw and send it off for a test. They have a doctor who comes over from Hutchinson two days a week. I told them I had gotten several blood transfusions and I was worried."

"And?"

"It came back negative. I had them do it again. Same thing. Nothing."

"Maybe the diagnosis in Denver was wrong."

"It wasn't. I had fourth and fifth opinions there. Believe me, I was running on fumes." Noah turned to face him in the gold of the prairie evening light. "I've had the test done every year since then. It's always clear."

Stern didn't know how to respond. Noah clearly believed that he had beaten the bug. Wasn't a carrier. Wasn't anything. Was cleanly negative. Though Stern knew that it was impossible, he prayed that it was true. He himself threw up every time he went in for the test, whenever he felt that there had been the slightest chance.... "That's amazing," he finally said. "What do you...?"

Noah bounded back onto the porch, waving his empty wineglass. "It's this place. It's this fucking place. It can't be anything else. I should have been dead fourteen years ago. It's this—*place*." His voice was fierce and certain. He leaned down and kissed Stern with a determination that sent his conscious mind reeling.

"I want you," Noah said. Stern nodded.

Noah's bedroom was upstairs, with windows facing the south and east, both of them open and screened, which meant that, as Stern lay naked on the bed, a cool cross breeze moved through the room and over his bare skin. The air smelled of distant rain, dust—and sex. And leather.

The sex had been slow, careful, and circumscribed because it had to be, with both their limitations. At least in Stern's mind it did. He had the desire, *god, he had the desire*, but not the need to penetrate or be penetrated. Not to leap into the void. He wished he had the faith in Noah to do more. He concentrated on memorizing the topography of Noah's body. This time it was Noah who was restrained, the straps wrapped and secured to the metal bed frame. It was Noah who wore the collar.

Stern licked, nibbled, stroked, and massaged over the seemingly vast landscape of wanting that was the skin, the terrain, of his lover. That this man had ever been sick was not an idea easily grasped. For Noah's part, he seemed content with stretching out naked with Stern's thigh flung across his own as he writhed against the straps. Kisses. Caresses. Visible orgasms onto fingers and flesh. All done without a sense of urgency, without the usual thoughtless lust. To Stern it was like they had discovered a new country. A place where there was time enough.

At a certain point during the night they arose and stumbled into the bathroom. Noah filled the ancient claw-footed tub with hot steamy water from the dying arterial aquifer below. The blood of the living earth. They bathed one another by touch, with only the blue glow of the rising moon through the small window. They sat in the cooling soapy water, nestled together, back to chest, Noah holding Stern in an embrace of both arms and legs.

"I thought I was giving all of this up," Noah said, and Stern knew what he meant. He had given *this* up as well. Out of fear and fatigue. Something occurred to him.

"You *never* leave this place do you? Not even for a single day."

"No, I haven't. Not in fifteen years. I'll never leave. That's the price, but it's an easy one. I love it here."

"You really do believe that?"

"Do I have any reason not to?"

Stern was silent for a long time. "No—no, you don't."

"Will you stay another day?"

"Yes. Another day won't matter," Stern stood and, stepping out of the tub, reached for a towel.

"It *will* definitely matter." One of Noah's hands emerged from the water and was on his hip, turning him around. Taking his flaccid cock into his mouth. Both of his hands kneaded Stern's buttocks. They were powerful hands, strengthened, Stern knew, by the work. He wondered what he really believed. Then every thought was overridden by white-hot pleasure and his cock grew and throbbed within the confines of Noah's mouth. The other man's palm suddenly slammed percussively against wet ass flesh, causing Stern to buck forward. Noah grinned up at him, pushing hips back until all but the head was showing outside of his lips. He slapped Stern's ass again.

"Put your hands on the sides of the tub and don't move them," Stern said. He pulled his cock entirely out of Noah's mouth. The other man looked confused, but did as he was told.

"We need some salt," Stern told him. "Stay just like that. I'll be right back." Thirty seconds later he was back from the bedroom, holding one leather binding-strap. With Noah kneeling in the tub, his hands clasping forearms behind his back, Stern bound the other man's limbs with leather. Buckled tight.

"Do you trust me?" Stern asked, thrusting forward. Noah responded by leaning in, accepting the cock fully. Stern dug his fingers into the thick coarse hair and fucked his mouth while they looked into one another's eyes. Never looking away. Trying not to even blink.

Stern stayed all of that day and the next—and the one after that. He called Boston and inquired as to how much of the job he could do by phone or email. He made up a story about a dying friend in Kansas. It turned out that the man preferred the distance. An empty bedroom at Noah's became Stern's office. He began revisions on a novel he had shelved, and accepted freelance editor-for-hire jobs that he had spurned in the past. It turned out that one *could* live in Kansas and have a life.

The leather was part of it. In sex—and in life. When Stern wasn't writing, he served as Noah's apprentice at the saddle shop. Hours were spent with wooden mallet and stamp, pounding intricate pebbled background textures into damp, thick tooling leather. Lacing saddles. Riveting silver-studded harnesses for the few remaining West Coast leather daddies. It turned out that there were still more than a few. Sometimes they played.

As the days passed and time flowed, Noah still asked him that same question almost every day. Stern always answered the same way. Stern knew that Noah loved him, partly because he *had* stayed. Stern began to learn to love the prairie, too, a sort of reconciliation with the landscape of his childhood. A place where the sky was too big and the horizon too long. A place where you couldn't hide from your fear or your dreams. He came to realize that it was never the land that he had hated, just the narrowness of acceptable opinion and experience.

In the late fall, Stern opened both doors on the barn and drove the MG inside, parking it in a space he had cleared against one wall. He put the top up and carefully covered the car with the canvas tarpaulin he had bought at the hardware store in town.

Finally, he plugged in the trickle charger he had installed to make sure the battery would always be up. He tucked half a dozen boxes of mouse and rat poison under the edges of the cover. Faith was one thing, foolishness another. The prairie winter would arrive soon.

WILLING

Xan West

I slam him against the wall. Bring out my knife. Whisper words across his skin, the steel teasing, tempting. Kick his legs apart, the blade ripping through his shirt, tormenting, aching to slice him open. Up close breathing on his neck, teeth almost breaking skin. Step back slapping, leaving a handprint on his cheek. My knife at his throat. My hand covering his mouth. My eyes on his. Feeding on his helplessness. Feeding on his fear. A slow smile creeping across my face as I begin. My fist driving into his pecs. My gloved hand slapping his face. His nipple twisted between my fingers, hot under my teeth. Turned around, face against the exposed brick of the wall. My fist on his back, methodical. My boot ramming into his ass. My open hand menacing him with slaps. My cock throbbing hard as I press into him and bite down on his shoulder, holding back, yet feeding on his pain. I ride with him as I pull out my tools, laying into his back...until I am ready to thrust the pain home with my quirt, driving welts into his back. We will soar together, gliding on his pain, his helplessness, my power, our pleasure. And when we are done flying, he will be on the floor at my feet, tongue wrapped around my boot.

It will do. The beast inside me calls for flesh, for pain. He is demanding and relentless and I barely keep him in check. It's better if they choose it. Want it. It adds a certain something that is indescribable and yet has become necessary to the meal. So I keep him sated with sadism, feeding on fear and pain and sex and helplessness. Once, I was waiting for the willing. That illusive willing boy I might call my own. I no longer hope for him. He does not exist.

Now, I find boys at the Lure. Boys like this one, who want to open themselves to my tools. But sometimes that is not enough to take the edge off. Sometimes it just stokes the hunger. When the urge for blood becomes uncontrollable I return to Gomorrah, looking for those hungry eyes, the pulse in a boy's throat that shows he wants it. It's hard to keep a straight face here, amidst the pretenders, the elitist pseudo-vampires, the Stand and Model version of S/M, the Sanguinarium, the followers of the Black Veil. So it's a last resort, this feast of image and fantasy. When the beast must feed and pain is not enough.

I come attired in simple, worn leather, well kept but understated, that moves fluidly with my body. I stride to a shadowed corner and watch for food. The rhythm of the music brings a booming to my brain as my eyes slide along the flesh exposed, watching for that look, that swiftly beating pulse in his throat.

Whispers begin as I am glimpsed by the regulars, and I know all it will take is a crook of my head and a smoldering gaze. It's too easy here. I am not seen. I am simply a fantasy come true, made all the more fantastic by my refusal to be showy in dress or demeanor. A growl of disgust rolls through me. I choose my meat, a tall, broad-shouldered goth boy with long black hair and a carefully trimmed beard. I draw him to me, and lead him out to the alley. He thinks this is a quick fuck, and drops to his knees. My hand grips him by that delicious hair and yanks him up, tossing him against the wall. I want to savor this meal. He needs to last.

I pull out my blade and show it to him. His eyes widen and he whispers, "My safeword is chocolate." I am surprised. Most who frequent the fetish scene know nothing about real BDSM. That these are the first words out of his mouth shows that there may be more to this boy than I thought. I stand still, watching him. He is older than I had first surmised, at least twenty-four. The little leather that he wears is well kept, his belt clearly conditioned, and his boots cared for by a loving hand. He is motionless, knees slightly bent, shoulders back, offering me his chest. His pulse is not rapid, but his eyes eat up the knife and his lips are slightly parted, as if all he wanted was to take my blade down his throat.

His brown eyes stay fixed on the knife as I move toward him. I tease his lip with the tip of it and then speak softly.

"How black do you flag?"

His eyes stay on the blade. He swallows.

"Very black, on the right, Sir."

"Is there anything I need to know?"

"I am healthy and strong. My limits are animals, children, suspension, and humiliation, Sir."

"And blood, hmmm?" I am teasing. I know the answer. It is why I found him here, and not at the Lure.

"Oh, please, Sir. I would gladly offer my blood."

"Why?"

He takes a deep breath, closes his eyes a moment, and then opens them. The pulse in his throat starts racing, but his voice is calm and matter-of-fact. I tease my blade against his neck.

"I have been watching you a long time, Sir. I have seen how

you play. I see the beast inside you. I know what is missing. Those boys at the Lure don't know how to give you what you really need. They don't see that they are barely feeding your craving, and not touching your hunger. The boys here don't see you. They just see their own fantasy. They are simply food. I am strong, Sir. Strong enough for you. I can be yours. My blood, my flesh, my sex, my service. Yours to take however you choose, for as long as you want. To slake your hunger. I would be honored, Sir."

I take a deep breath, stunned, studying him. This boy who would offer what I never really thought was possible. He has surprised me again. That alone shows this boy is more than a meal. He just might be able to be all that he has offered.

I almost leave him there. I am ready to walk away. Fear creeps along my spine. With the centuries I have lived and the things I have seen, this boy is what scares me. There is nothing more terrifying than hope. I rake my eyes over him. He is standing quietly. He looks as if he could stand in that position for hours. He has said his piece; he is content to wait for my response. Oh, he is more than food, this one. What a gift to offer a vampire. Can I refuse this offering when it's laid out before me? I step back, looking him over, and decide.

I breathe in possibility, watching the pulse in his throat. My senses heighten further as I focus my hunger on him, noticing the minute changes in breath, scenting him. I want to see him tremble. I want to smell his fear. I want to devour his pain, without holding back. Forget this public arena. If there is even a possibility that I might truly let go and move with the beast inside my skin, his growl on my lips and his claws grasping prey, I know exactly where I need to take this boy.

I put the knife away, pull the black handkerchief from his back pocket, and wrap it around his head, covering his eyes. He cannot see the way to where we are going. He has not earned that much trust. I grip him by the back of the neck and lead him to my bike. When I start the engine, its growl answers me, echoing off the walls of the alley. I take the long way, through twists and turns of the backstreets, enjoying the wind on my face and the purr of the bike.

We are here. I ease him off the bike and lead him by the neck down the stairs into the lower level of the brownstone. It is a large soundproof room. There are no windows. It is one big tomb. Every detail is designed for my pleasure, down to the exposed brick wall installed for the simple gratification of slamming meat against it. This room is where I sleep and where I take my prey when I want privacy. Private play means I let my hair down and roam free, claws unsheathed. I leave him in the doorway and ready myself, breathing deep, freeing my hair. I strip off my shirt so I can feel hair brush my lower back. It is my vanity, and I have worn it long for centuries, no matter the current fashion.

I keep him blindfolded, and throw him against the wall. There is a ritual about it, beginning with a wall and a knife. It communicates the road we are on. He is trapped, with nowhere to run. He is pressed against the wall, and going to take any impact into his body, through it to the wall, and back again, driven in a second time. He is facing danger, sharp edges. He could be torn open. He is pressed against something rough and hard. He is still. I am moving. He cannot see what's coming. My knife breaks the unspoken rules of knife play, and goes to places that feel forbidden and fraught with more danger than expected. And my knife shows my need. You can hear it in my breathing, feel it surge through my body. It travels the air in electric bursts of energy.

I play with it, toying with him, ramping my need up through

his fear. I slap his face with the large blade. I run it along the top of his eye, just under the blindfold, teasing it against his eyelid, so he knows just how easy it would be to burst the eyeball. I fuck him with it, thrusting the tip under his jaw, not breaking skin, just teasing my cock to hardness at the thought of thrusting it deep. There's a catch in his breath as I draw his lower lip down and slide the blade along it. My mouth swoops in out of nowhere and bites down on that lip, just barely breaking skin. This is a test of my control, as I slowly lick the fruit I have exposed and growl deep in my throat. He is hypnotically delicious, his blood electric in a way that is familiar and yet surprising. I grip his throat in my hand, constricting his breath, watching his face, his mouth. It is true. He has surprised me again. I tuck my new knowledge and my surprise away, knowing that I can do my worst. Folks always said that his kind make good boys for us. Perhaps I will be able to test that tonight. I release his throat and watch him breath deeply. I grip his hair and tilt his head back.

"Keep your mouth open and still."

I start to tease it in, watching the large black blade slide into his throat. I exhale loudly. He is motionless for me, breath held, taking my knife. My cock jumps at the sight, as I start to fuck his throat. Mine. This incredible wave of possessiveness roars through me as I thrust into him. And I want to see his eyes. I tear through the blindfold with my teeth, the blade still lodged in his throat, and meet his gaze. His eyes are shimmering, large, and full…full of what? I thrust in deeper, watching his pupils dilate with…is that joy? I can feel his heart race, see him struggle as he realizes he needs to breathe. He must exercise perfect control, and not move his mouth or throat as he exhales and then takes in his first breath. Fear fills him. Not because he is afraid of the knife. Because he knows that it would displease me to draw blood when I don't intend to, and his whole being is focused on pleasing me. He works to do it perfectly, and contentment washes over his face as he succeeds. I thrust deeper in appreciation, picturing his throat muscles working to avoid contact with the blade. Oh, this will be fun. I slide out of his throat.

I want my claws on his chest, now. I want to rip him open, expose him to my gaze, my teeth, my hunger. I want his blood on every tool in my possession. Now. I want to feast on him. I can feel the beast roll through my body.

Not yet. I want more pain to draw it out. I want to see if it's true. I want to know he can take my worst and still want more. I want to see his strength. That is worth delaying my feed. And postponing it will only make it sweeter.

I breathe deeply, focusing my senses as I walk slowly in front of him, inspecting him from every angle. He straightens his posture, easing into a position he can hold. I pull on my leather gloves and move close, gripping his shirt, tearing it swiftly from his chest and tossing it onto the floor. That's what I want first. I throw my shoulder into the body-slam and feel the electricity of our skins' contact. I trace my fingertips along the horizontal scars on his chest and then grip his nipples, twisting. I am so close. I cannot resist sinking my teeth in and teasing myself. I bite deeply, barely avoiding breaking skin. Building connection. Making my cock throb. Drawing out my beast. I lift up and bite down, feeling his body shift with the pain, laying my mark on him. I claim him like this, first. Begin in the way you wish to proceed. With fear and pain and teeth and sex all rolled together. I can feel the blood pulsing just at the surface, calling me. I bite down hard and thrust my cock against him. My low growl mixes with the slow, soft moan that escapes his lips. I lift my head to meet his eyes, and see that he has begun to fly.

I step back and begin my dance around him. Heaving my fist into his chest. My boot into his thigh. My open hand slamming down onto his pecs. I move rapidly, layering and shifting, gliding around him. Thrusting pain into him in unpredictable gusts of movement. Upping the ante. Ramming my boot into his cock, grinding the heel in and watching his eyes. He is twirling high in the air, lips parted, offering himself to me. His eyes entreat me to use him. And I do. Exercising minute control, I coil into him, watching as he floats. This is just the beginning. I constrict his breath, cover his mouth and nose so all he breathes is leather, and thrust my teeth into his shoulder, feeling his heart against my tongue.

I lead him to the table and tell him to remove what he must to give me access to his ass. He takes off his pants and socks, folding them neatly and stacking them on top of his boots in the corner. He is wearing a simple leather jock. I order him facedown on the table. He is quivering. *Mine,* I think. And catch myself. I watch him, building on his fear, and remove my touch. There is only the knife sliding along him, forcing him to remain still. There is only the knife, as silence lies on him like a blanket. I step away, moving quietly, and leave him alone. We will see how much he needs connection, how much fear I can build. We will see, I think slowly to myself, how much distance I can tolerate.

My play is usually about connection. About driving myself inside. About opening someone up to my gaze. My tools are up close and personal. Play is my source of connection, and I usually hurl into it, deep and hard. I don't want to show myself yet. This must be done slowly. I want to see what he can do. I want to wait, before I commit myself to what I have already thought. I will come to that on my terms, in my time.

I fetch my favorite canes, needing air between us. Needing that sound that whips through the air and blasts into flesh. Needing controlled, careful cruelty. Canes are a special love of mine. It takes a lot for me to risk thin sticks of wood, easily broken to form deadly weapons. Canes are about my risk, too. Their simple existence menaces. Their joy is unmatchable.

I line up my weapons on a nearby table, carefully. Thinking ahead, I select another item and place it on the table, softly. I am ready.

I step back, allowing the necessary distance, and begin from stillness. I place my stripes precisely, just slow enough for him to get the full ripping effect of the bite. I lay lines of piercing sting, not holding back my strokes, saturating him with an invasive assault. There is nothing like the sound of a cane mutilating air, and he shivers at it. I can feel the fear rising off him like steam and breathe it in as my due. I am unforgiving. It will never end. I can loom over him, layering slashes on skin, for eternity. I am breathing deeply. This is meditative. And I realize though there is air and space between us, I am attuned to his breathing. My cock swells at the almost imperceptible sounds he makes. We are connected. There is no breaking that. I know that he could be halfway across the country and I would feel the pulse of his blood. I smile at the thought, accepting it. I am ready. Ready to rend his skin with my teeth and tools. To break him open and take a good long taste. To unleash the beast roaming in my skin.

I feel an incredible calm at the roaring in my blood. A new calm. I can fully be who I am in this room, with this man. He is strong enough. And I trust him enough to risk. I pick up my belt, and begin.

There are few tools I have a deeper connection with. I have had this leather belt since the nineteenth century, and cared for it well. It is a part of me. An extension of my cock and my will. Nothing brings out my beast like my belt. Which is why I keep it at home, and only use it on prey I am going to devour. Until now.

I explain this to him, watching him tremble.

"Please use me, Sir," is all he says.

Mine. Possessiveness washes over me. I double the belt and start slamming him with it, the welts rising rapidly. Vision begins to blur. This is all about sound and movement. My body senses where to strike. My blows hammer him into the table. I can feel a growl building in my throat as his scent shifts. My cock swells, as I hurl the leather into his back in rapid, crashing surges.

"Mine," I growl. "Mine to hurt. Mine to use. Mine to feed on. Mine."

The possessiveness rises in me, a tsunami cresting and breaking over him as I blast the belt into his back, rending his skin. Welts form on top of welts and break the surface. He is moaning as I howl, the beast fully in my skin and oh so hungry. I lay the belt across the back of his neck and crouch on the table above him, eyes focused on the gashes opening his back to me. I drop on top of him, rubbing my chest into the blood on his back.

I breathe in the scent of him and growl happily, "Mine."

I free my cock, swollen to bursting, and shed my pants. I will savor the first real taste. Right now, it's enough to smell it and feel it against my skin, and know there is more for the taking. I rub it onto my cock, stroking it in as I close my eyes. I want inside, now. Want to rend him open. Thrust myself into him, bloody and hard. I want to tear his back open with claws and teeth, and feast.

I describe this to him, and he moans his consent.

"Please, Sir," he says softly. "Please."

He is all want and need and craving, and where his hunger meets mine we will crest. Mine. The word fills me, taking me over.

I thrust into him, my cock smeared in his blood, ramming into his ass for my pleasure. He is so open for me, so willing.

His groans are loud and true as I fuck him, rubbing my face in the blood on his back. I grip his hips, and stop, embedded in him. I can feel my claws extend right before I slash into his back, ripping him open. The blood flows freely and I bathe my chest in it, bellowing as I hurl my cock into him. I wrap the belt around his neck, constricting his breath, my cock pounding him into the table, and I bite. Mulled wine. Spicy. Sweet. Tangy. I drink him down, savoring each gulp, thrusting steadily. I release his neck, hear his gasping breaths, and bite harder, feeding.

"Please, Sir," he manages in a throaty whisper.

I lift my head. "Please what, boy?"

This is the first time I have called him "boy," and he whimpers at the sound of it.

"Please, Sir. Please may I come, Sir?"

I thrust into him hard, and feel his ass grab me.

"Mine. You are my boy. Mine to fuck. Mine to slash open. Mine to devour. Mine to mark. Mine to command. You may come when I sink my teeth into you again, boy. I want to hear it. Tell me you are mine, and then you may come."

I drive my cock into him, reaming him deeply, and rub my chest against his bloody back. I reach around to grab his cock, gripping it tightly and stroking it in quick bursts. I plunge my teeth into his shoulder. Gnawing him open. Snarling as I drink. My dick pumping into him.

"I am yours, Sir. I offer myself freely for your use. I am so glad to be yours, Sir."

I explode into him, storms crashing in huge tidal waves. Drinking and coming. Releasing myself and drawing him in. His ass clenches around me in spasms as he bursts, his body bucking and shuddering. I continue to feed. When his body calms, I am sated, and I ease myself out of him slowly. I take my time licking his wounds closed, savoring the taste of him. I pull him up into my arms, smiling.

"Now let's see that cock of yours, boy."

His eyes go wide, he looks down, and he starts trembling again. I lift his chin to meet his eyes, and then trace the scars on his chest lightly with my tongue. I lift my head to stare into his eyes again, and slowly unzip the jock, revealing a large black silicone cock. I pump it hard, stroking it against him, where I know he is enlarged by testosterone.

"Did you think I didn't know, boy? After all the centuries I've lived, did you think I did not learn how to read people?"

I grin into his eyes.

"You are my boy. And I am proud to claim you as mine."

I gather him to me, holding him tight, and start imagining possibilities.

QUIS CUSTODIET IPSOS CUSTODES?

Karl von Uhl

Master Richard was very particular about who he invited to his functions. This one, in particular, was to be no ordinary orgy. He wanted everyone to enjoy himself, and would brook no observers. That was one of the rules: there are no observers, only participants. To hell with the voyeurs. He had no use for voyeurs. Watching wasn't a fetish, and it certainly wasn't kinky.

Leather wasn't a fetish, either. Leather was a way of life. For Master Richard and his enclave of playmates, leather was held in high esteem. It wasn't simply something they put on. Leather was earned. There were dues to be paid, respect to be earned, and dedication to be proved. Leather was not taken lightly. Leather was, literally, skin for skin.

Master Richard was particular, too, about selecting the day. Fridays were out, because that's when everyone wanted to drink and party. Wednesdays were bad because too many sex clubs had Wednesday night specials. Tuesday was for Tuesday Sucks. Thursday was for the Bare Chest Contest. So he chose a Saturday, typically a date night, for this event, and made sure his attendees knew far enough in advance to make the night available.

For tonight's initiate, a young man named Ryan, Master Richard had invited John, Wade, Simon, and Terry to assist. The five waited for Ryan, enthusiastic for the evening's entertainment, and greeted him, Master Richard at the focus of their semicircle, when he arrived.

"Who're these guys?" asked Ryan, affable yet apprehensive, when Master Richard let him in. John, Wade, Simon, and Terry, each shirtless in a top's harness and leather pants, held a quirt, a cane, a paddle, and a cat, respectively.

"The four leathermen of the apocalypse," said Master Richard. He shut the door.

"Oh, god," said Ryan, clad in denim and army boots, honestly afraid.

"God won't help you here," said Simon, who slapped his paddle against his thigh as punctuation.

"Strip," said Master Richard. Ryan moved as quickly as possible, not wanting to displease the men. When he was naked, Master Richard said, "Through there," and pointed to the middle room of his flat.

The room was painted black, and with the pocket doors closed, the effect was engagingly claustrophobic. There were naked red bulbs in the fixtures, which were adjusted by rheostats to further mute the light. Ryan stood at the room's center between two chains that hung from the ceiling, hovering about eight inches over his shoulders. Wade and Terry went in, clipped restraints to the chains in tandem, and bound Ryan's arms. Ryan's cock was half hard.

"Who told you to get a hard-on?" said Wade, landing his cane sharply on Ryan's smooth ass. Ryan hissed at its touch, which left a thin red stripe.

"Tonight, we invite another into our midst," said Master Richard, "into our everlasting chain of men." John blindfolded Ryan. Master Richard strode in front of him. "These men know I've been training you," he said. "They know precisely what you can take and what you think you can take. Tonight, you will become one of us." Ryan shivered, tried to regain his balance.

Terry plugged in a set of clippers, clicked them on. He placed them against a tuft of hair at Ryan's throat and neatly buzzed it away. Ryan stood stock-still, with his knees slightly bent. Master Richard, John, Wade, and Simon left the room and strode up the hall to the kitchen. Each helped himself to a Bud from the refrigerator.

" 'Everlasting chain of men'?" asked Simon.

"I read it in a dirty story," said Master Richard. "It just sounded good. Sort of ritualistic."

"Where ever did you find him?" asked Wade.

"He's a grad student at Stanford. Feminist studies, of all things," said Master Richard. "I think he has a minor in psychology."

"Shame all that hair has to come off," said John.

"You and body hair," said Simon. "You like those hairy guys so much. You can have them."

"It's because he's smooth," said Master Richard. "Right, John?"

"That's part of it, I guess," said John. "I just always liked the way hairy guys looked. I remember I had a real hairy uncle I liked."

"I just bet you liked him," said Simon.

"Like you wouldn't love to collect more jack-off material," said John. "Nothing happened. Ever."

"Ever?" asked Simon.

"It's the real world. Nothing happens in the real world."

In the playroom, hair continued to fall from Ryan's chest, then his belly and armpits. Terry took a quick look at Ryan's back; there was a small patch of hair just above his ass. *That'll have to go,* he thought.

He put down the clippers and went rummaging through a toy chest. After a few moments, he found a respectably sized butt plug, greased it up, and shoved it in Ryan's ass. Ryan cried out, either in surprise or pain—it didn't especially matter to Terry. He resumed clipping, watching as Ryan's fine pubes piled up on the floor. "Spread wider," he said. Ryan opened his legs and Terry trimmed the hair on his perineum. Terry knew the butt plug was vibrating sympathetically with the clippers.

Terry made quick work of Ryan's legs, the fine, fair hair littering the floor as the clippers passed. He clicked the clippers off and, kneeling, admired his work: Ryan looked very good clipped down, his skin more pink than pale, his pencil-eraser nipples small and pointed amid the stubble. He'd look even better completely smooth, thought Terry.

Terry opened an armoire and removed a stainless steel bowl, shaving cream, and a disposable razor. He opened his fly and pissed into the bowl.

He returned to Ryan. "Piss," he ordered. Ryan didn't do anything. Terry smacked the back of his head, open palmed. "Piss!" Still nothing. "Okay. I'm gonna put this bowl on the floor," said Terry, knocking the bowl on the hard wood, "and if you miss it, I'm gonna kick your ass." Then he picked up the bowl carefully, so as not to make a sound, and held it a few feet from Ryan's cock.

Ryan breathed deep and slow, trying to relax. After a few moments, a few droplets of piss squirted from his cock. Terry caught them in the bowl. Ryan, relieved to hear liquid on steel, let his stream flow harder, though it still seemed inhibited. Probably the plug, thought Terry. When Ryan was through, Terry said, "Good boy," and left the room.

He went up the hall to the kitchen. The others stopped talking and watched as Terry walked to the sink and ran some hot water into the bowl. Terry turned, regarded all of them with raised eyebrows, and went back to the playroom.

Terry splashed the water-piss mixture on Ryan, used it to wet down his chest and crotch. The smell was the important thing for Terry; he wanted Ryan to know he had been marked, even after the hair grew back. Terry squirted shaving cream into his palm and smeared it liberally over Ryan's torso.

When the razor touched him, Ryan flinched but made no sound. Terry worked swiftly to remove the stubble the clippers had left behind, shaving in short, rapid strokes, slicing sweet trails of smooth skin through the white cream. Terry was tempted to cut him, but knew that was off limits. *Another time,* he thought, but Terry knew Ryan would look damn hot streaked with cat scratches.

When he reached Ryan's crotch, Terry got a new razor. Sometimes pubic hair was tougher, and he wanted a fresh blade. He pinched the head of Ryan's cock, lifting the shaft out of his way as he shaved clean the place where it joined Ryan's crotch. Then he grasped Ryan's scrotum, pulled the skin taut and shaved it slowly. This was one of Terry's favorite parts: the sharp blade against what was truly the measure of a man. *One slip of the blade is all it would take,* he thought. One deliberate move and his tender balls would be history. But that was for another time. For Ryan, shaving was castration enough. Terry lamented not having a straight razor.

He held the balls high against Ryan's belly, shaved his perineum. *When it grows back, the itching will make him crazy,* thought Terry. Not like your balls itching, Terry knew; this was an itch you could never scratch genteelly.

Last was Ryan's plugged butthole. Again, a new razor was used for this, the softest of skin. Terry carefully stroked the hair off, leaving Ryan with a shiny, pinkish-brown pucker. Terry fought the desire to rim him, to taste Ryan's hole and his own smooth handiwork.

Terry stood, swatted Ryan's ass hard. "I'm done," he said. "But you're not." He left the room, taking the bowl and razors down the hall to the kitchen.

"Next!" he shouted, loud enough to be heard by Ryan.

"Jeez, Terry, tell the neighborhood," said Master Richard.

"Like they don't know who lives here," said Terry, grabbing a Bud from the refrigerator, "or what goes on."

"Anything I should know?" asked Simon.

"I plugged him," said Terry.

"Back in a bit, gentlemen," said Simon, brandishing his paddle as he left.

John leaned forward. "Hell, I've seen him in a full bridle, let alone a bit," he said, in something of a stage whisper, when Simon was gone. The men laughed.

"When did you see Simon in a bridle?" asked Wade, eager for gossip.

"During a trip to New York. I don't think he was expecting to see anyone he knew."

"And you?"

Nodding his head, John said, "It was hot. It was real hot."

"Was it an animal trip or something?" asked Master Richard.

"No. I always thought he was bicoastal, and I just got my proof, is all."

"Only the best bottoms make it to the top," said Master Richard, repeating aloud what they all took as a de facto article of faith: surely, this is what everyone knows. "I'm most assuredly a top, but I know what my ass is for," continued Master Richard. Down the hall, the solid foursquare tattoo of a wooden paddle against skin began.

"Not me. Mine's for rimming only," said John. He took a swig from his bottle.

"You just never found the right guy to fuck you," said Master Richard.

"Oh, yeah, right. Like I never found the right woman to make me straight, either," said John, smiling. Down the hall, Ryan yelped, but the paddling accelerated, then stopped momentarily.

"Trust me on this one. You can't say never in S/M," said Master Richard.

"Yeah, I've heard it before. But I don't think the right man is out there."

"It's all sensation. You have to explore it before you know if you're going to be into it," said Terry. "That's how I got into water sports." He took a pull on his Bud. "I was taking a bath one day and had to piss. Rather than stand up and use the toilet I just pissed right there. In the tub." Terry was steeped in guilelessness. "And then I looked down and saw I had this absolutely incredible hard-on." He took another slug of beer.

"I'm pretty sure I don't need to shit myself to know I'm not into it," said John. "No offense, Terry."

"None taken," said Terry.

"But I know what you mean. You have to have fantasies," said John, a little contrite. "If you don't have fantasies, then what have you got to make into reality?"

Ryan yelped again. This time there was no break in the paddling.

"Fantasies are the safest of all. And strictly speaking, S/M is safe sex, anyway," said Master Richard. "So we've been safe all these years." He paused for a drink. "Beating the crap out of each other," he said, smiling.

"I've never known a top to get it," said Terry.

"No, it's a top's disease, too," said Wade.

"I dunno," said Terry. He took another swig of Bud. "People are dating now, and I suppose that's good."

"This is a date of sorts," said Master Richard. "A group date."

Wade laughed. "A group date? You're such a product of the fifties. So wholesome."

Master Richard smiled, bowed his head.

"Well, I do know that you can't find tops and bottoms like you used to," said Terry.

"Absolutely," said Master Richard, pulling himself upright, as if irate that he'd been unaware of his slouching. "I don't know what's gotten into these younger people, but they don't know what they're doing. Just going in and working each other over."

Ryan cried out sharply and the paddling stopped. The men could hear Ryan's ragged breathing turn into sobs.

John smiled, satisfied. "That always gets me hard," he said. "When a man cries."

Wade groped him. "Sentimental you," he said, patting John's thickening cock.

"You know, I think that's the only fluid we can share now," said John.

"What?" asked Wade, settling himself against the kitchen counter.

"Tears," said John.

"Tears and piss," said Terry, matter-of-factly. "Piss is safe." They heard the paddling resume.

"These young people, they confuse everything," said Master Richard.

"And none of them want to join the clubs," said Terry.

"No, of course not, they can't be bothered," said Master Richard.

"The clubs will always be there," said Wade.

"Not if nobody joins them," said Terry.

"So what can be done to get these young'uns involved?" asked John, semi-facetiously, bored with the turn of conversation.

"We need to talk to them," said Master Richard. "We need to show them how it's done, like what we're doing with Ryan here tonight. We need to get to them before they hurt someone." He took a final swig from his bottle and put it down. "And before they hurt themselves. Otherwise we'll lose them entirely. They'll be gone and no good to anyone."

"And before we're gone," said John, meaning to be playful, but more sarcastically than he intended.

"Absolutely. You're absolutely right, John," said Master Richard, oblivious.

"You know what I don't get? The clothing. How everything is baggy now," said Terry. "It's absolutely antisex. It's so sex-negative."

Simon padded into the room. He always walked quietly, even with heavy boots. "He's been welted nicely on his ass. Give him a moment or two to recover," he said, "and then I think it's your turn." He looked at John.

John brandished his quirt. "I can do that," he said, setting his eyebrows and jaw as if to form a mask. "I am hungry like the wolf."

HOW A GUY ON A BIKE CAN GET HIT BY A CAR, MADE TO EAT ASPHALT, AND THANK GOD ALL THE WHILE

horehound stillpoint

This man...oh man...he's sexy as a Hollywood version of Hell...smart as Sartre...easy to respect as a geodesic dome, and funny as rimming might look to a Martian.

Now I've traded blow jobs with a LOT of guys, and after a creamy orgasm or two, most of them start chatting about real estate in Northern California, vacations in European steam rooms, memberships in straight versus gay gyms, Madonna's genius...or the latest Cher impersonation perpetrated by Cher. This new guy—the one I'm amazed to find myself seeing—he opens up about the work he's doing in Afghanistan, as a volunteer. He's helping to renovate an old palace and turn it into a school (with nine hundred rooms) so that the children can learn their arts and their crafts in order to keep this bombed-to-shit country from losing its beautiful and unique culture. Important stuff. And he does it in spite of his coworkers, who not only fail to support him but who mock him and think he's slightly retarded for going over to...wait, where was it again?

Iran? (We Americans have so much trouble remembering which of those countries is which.) He does it in spite of the discomfort involved, and the loss of money he incurs and in spite of the fact that his own government, especially the FBI, now considers him a probable enemy, just because he dared to visit that part of the world.

He's sharing all this while snapping his leather jockpiece back into place, then pulling on a pair of long johns (if there's a sexier garment made by man, I want to see it), then even my soul is on its knees, moaning, ejaculating...exclaiming three little words which change everything...thank you, God, thank you, God, Thank...You...God.

Thank you, God for the whole fucking world, even if it isn't big enough to contain my joy, and for the sky that gives my mind room to breathe...for bodies of water that make it seem like it will be okay to die. Thank you for the Earth...the fundamental place of roots...the ground of luminosity rising...for all the varieties of love as it manifests in the concrete Cosmos of atoms and cells and seconds and thoughts creating isolation. Hallelujah! Isolation is what presents us with opportunities to come together...and we have, this new guy and I...come together. Oh, yes.

Thank you, God for proving that, in spite of my past, and my outrageously confused and possibly pathetic present condition, I am still capable of full-on romantic...love. I don't know what else to call it, when I find myself, at work, singing, "You're just too good to be true..."

I haven't thought of that song in almost forty years, but he cut right through my aging exterior, my Punk Rock 70s Heavy Metal–dedicated periphery; my shiny, black, candy-coated, outer shell. Bless his strong leathery heart. And I thank all the Gay Saints in Heaven for his sturdy cock...his overloaded balls...

his tight, tender ass…those carefully calibrated fingers of his working my nipples to the nth degree…his determined tongue, darting everywhere…his knee-melting eyes…all the things he uses to penetrate the defenses that have accumulated around my core since the beginning of rock 'n' roll, being that I was born in the year "Rock Around the Clock" was written. Much, much shit has happened in the meantime; there's been spilled milk, broken bones, broken hearts, blood everywhere; water under the bridge, carrying the flotsam and jetsam of decades; tons of pollution.

We've been from that war to this war, from blotter acid to antidepressants, and I'm still trying to process the death of all but one of the original Ramones. Before this new guy came along, I didn't even remember I used to like Frankie Valli.

He's gotten so deeply inside me, even though he hasn't actually fucked me yet…nor I him. We will, of course. I mean, I hope we will. My ass is still in good shape because of all the biking I do on the hills of San Francisco, not to mention hours and hours of yoga every week; his is in great shape because he's African American, walks everywhere, and hits the gym regularly. It's just that we're both tops. Mostly. He said he can't wait for me to fuck him…but he said it right after we had both come. He's in no hurry and neither am I. Getting fucked is not my favorite sex act. It's not even in my top five, honestly. Guys want to fuck me, try to fuck me; a few have even pleaded their cases with great persuasion. But, really, I only want to get fucked when I'm starting to fall for a guy, when I think we have a chance in hell of being inside each other's lives as much as inside each other's hot, slicked-up asses. That's when I open up: when I can feel the love in the room for real. I have made exceptions…when I felt as if my Gay Card was in danger of being taken away. I figure, the world being what it is, I better have a nice juicy cock up my butt at least once in a blue moon, to straighten out my shit. So to speak.

Anyone seeing this new guy and me walking down Folsom Street together, well, at least nine out of ten people would guess that he was the top in the relationship. I look like a bottom, act like a bottom, and I like to be on the bottom while some hot stud is riding my dick...playing with my balls...and my nipples...maybe he's jerking himself off...or we're kissing and grinding up against each other like it's the end of the world. But my new guy and I haven't gotten around to that yet. We're both happy, sweaty, and satisfied sticking to oral. He likes to pull me over to him while he's in a chair...or he gets on his knees and takes my dick in his mouth, inch by inch. He takes his time about it. Damn, he's got me convinced I have ten inches. Or more! I'm busting out of my old measurements. He tit-tortures me just enough. He never hurries. He's never in a rush to get his dick into the action. He stays hard anyway. I lean against a wall, a table, a door, and let him go to town. I know I'll get my turn to go down. His dick is juicy, meaty, musty, and selfish enough to be utterly convincing. I flat-out love his balls. Never tasted better. Never felt a more shapely pair up against my chin.

He is one Salty Dog. He would have been a sailor, fifty years ago, back when sailors were hot, perfectly built, naturally masculine, worldly wise, somewhat weary, and very queer. Ready to do whatever job was in front of him. Also, ready to smirk, at the drop of a hat.

Of course I'll let the new guy fuck me. When we get there.

In the bigger picture, I recognize the ridiculous unfairness of two tops getting together, considering the number of bottoms in San Francisco and the relative scarcity of tops. Maybe we'll end up getting married and turn into one of those couples who ride around in an Explorer picking up bottoms for us both to use and abuse and then kick to the curb...with delirious grins on their cherubic but mischievous faces. That's how I got into my first three-way, back in the days of Queen, Bowie, Mott the Hoople, and Roxy Music. There were these two guys, down in Monterey, who used to ride around in a van...they patrolled an area the size of Rhode Island in search of cute and available bottoms. They got me into their van, one fine afternoon, and I will testify that it is huge fun, being the boy meat in a man sandwich. One was a blond, ex-farmboy from the Midwest; I fucked him. The other was an Italian guy from New York City, he fucked me while I was fucking blondie. Whew. Turned me out, I must admit. I don't remember their names.... I did tell my long-term lover (at the time) about the experience, since we were nonmonogamous and he said, "Oh, you mean Hatchet-Head and Stubble? They tried to pick me up, too, ya know. That's all those guys do, drive around looking for unsuspecting tricks. They take turns fucking 'em left, right, and sideways, and then you never see 'em again."

I thought our relationship could have maybe used a bit of that action. But Michael and I had already been together for five years, and knowing him the way I did, I kept my own counsel.

Or perhaps, since this new guy works for a major leather store, we could initiate the penetration stage of our relationship with a re-creation of my absolutely favorite night of "two-tops-taking-turns-screwing-each-other," when that boyfriend of some years ago loaned me one of his two pairs of custom-made leather shorts. He wore the other pair. Both had holes in the rear and holes in the front; we went through some rubbers that night. He liked putting a dot of Tiger Balm in the lube. Man, it got hot! Those leather shorts got so sweaty...we fucked each other all night long. He was from German stock, with the meatiest thighs, a cock thick enough to serve for dinner, an ass so high and round, porn companies begged him to come to their studios. But he was like me: he just wanted to give it away. Felt so good being inside him...on top of those supermasculine haunches... him squeezing the hell out of my cock and balls. Once again, what was or is there to say, then as now, but thank you, God.

Thank you for my body, this vehicle of experience...this body mind heart and soul thing, which greets me faithfully every morning...loving and loyal as the dog I had growing up. Always there. Always playful, even in the midst of difficulty. I've had my share of disease and suffering...loss and grief...unbelievable betrayal. We have tried to get rid of each other, at times, this body and I, when my body tortured my mind too much, or vice versa. Yet it still serves, it gets around, it shows me new sights... new lips to savor...new buns to caress. I just follow my nose and kiss whatever or whoever is in front of me...kiss lick suck spit and/or swallow.

Even when I am disappointed, in pain, crushed, defeated, dispirited, just through with the whole fucking world...something of me remains. Some mysterious core of gratitude hangs on...waiting, breathing, shining...invisible and undeniable...not only okay, but glad.

I'm more than okay with God making me the kind of guy (slut) who will follow an intriguing man anywhere, anytime, under any pretense...because you never really know what will happen when you go to your local leather store to replace a favorite old neoprene cock ring. A guy can meet the man of his dreams...come face-to-face with real-time fantasy...at any moment. That's how I met this guy, dashing into a store, to make a five-minute, ten-dollar purchase.

And there he was. Smiling.

Friendly.

Interested.

Obviously, we are still in the Age of Miracles, and never mind what the scientific evidence of the everyday world seems to suggest.

So...

Thank you, God for making the new man's body ABSolutely perfect...with his bulging arms...treasure chest...thighs of heavy, curvy, creamy muscle...his statuesque bearing...lips made for so much more than talking and eating...and eyes full of gentleness and better worlds and happier children and braver adults...just looking into those eyes makes me feel more fully human.

Thank you, God for my new man's ability to communicate, not to mention his willingness to be transcendentally blown away by the poetry of my great friend Trebor Healey. What a refreshing change, after my previous boyfriends, tricks, lovers, and husbands, most of whom having nothing to say after hearing five minutes of poetry except "Good-bye" (from a trick), or "Can we order a pizza now?" (from a lover). To be fair, two or three of these were pretty good at communicating their hopes and insecurities, their emotions and spiritual progress. But still...he's one in a million. And I am one of the few human beings alive with the numbers under my belt to back that supposition up.

In the evening, after one of his visits, I find myself thanking God for a car that came out of nowhere, knocking me and my bicycle over...because that's how happy I am...in this moment. Thanks for another opportunity to crash...thanks for all the mistakes I've made...thanks for my whole ridiculous life, which has taught me how to fall flat on my face. Thanks for this asphalt in my kisser. Thanks for all the men who swept me off my feet and then just let me fall...in love...with love...out of lust and into the fire. I don't know anything but how to fall...and, without knowing how I know, how to rise. This is what we do in love:

we rise and fall...we unfold...we get hard...we melt, we stretch, and the Universe expands.

Thank you, God for every opportunity for enlightenment... yes, even right here, right now. Nothing exists but consciousness. Nothing exists but love. Nothing exists but joy...nothing but God...nobody but God...no one but God. Thank you, God, you are everywhere. He is here. At last. The new man is come and I am found.

IN THE SHADOW OF DEVIL'S BACKBONE

Jeff Mann

For Kent, with thanks for Highland

> *Come live with me and be my love,*
> *And we will all the pleasures prove,*
> *That hills and valleys, dales and field,*
> *And all the craggy mountains yield.*
> —Christopher Marlowe,
> "The Passionate Shepherd to His Love"

I

Raucous redneck shouts, Bud Light, and potato chips: that's how this long-awaited weekend begins, here in Staunton, Virginia, in Rick's modest living room. The Hokies are playing William and Mary today, a bright, warm October afternoon, so before our boys head up to the cabin in that high, distant mountain cove, they've got to catch the televised football game.

Rick and Walker could be any two sports fans, except for what they're wearing. When they don their leathers, that begins their ritual, their religion, their transformation. It signifies that the most crucial and beautiful aspect of the weekend—Rick's dominance, Walker's submission—has begun.

Rick's sprawled comfortably in the big armchair before the TV. He's dressed in jeans and black harness-strap boots, and he's bare chested, except for a black leather bar vest that frames the red body hair he's so proud of. The curly fur softens the hard curves of his pecs, ridges his flat belly, and disappears below his belt, a thick strap of buffed leather that will soon serve a sacramental purpose.

Rick's well muscled from his weekly work, hauling heavy antiques around the auction house. His skin is freckled and pale, his goatee's bushy, just a few shades darker than his body hair. There's a black leather biker's cap cocked over his brow, a treat he allowed himself the last time he sidestepped life in Virginia long enough to make it to the Folsom Street Fair.

Walker's on his knees on the floor at Rick's feet, hands clasped behind his back as ordered. He's even better built than Rick, due to obsessive gym devotion—lean waist, toned torso, and muscle-plump arms—but his chest and belly are shaved smooth, as is his scalp. Unlike Rick, he's well tanned from working shirtless in his garden, literally rednecked after hours spent hoeing corn, not to mention his days working on the road crew or motorcycling around the Shenandoah Valley. He's big shouldered and narrow hipped, a few years younger than Rick's thirty-five, an inch shorter than Rick's five foot nine.

Walker's sporting a light brown soul patch; silver hoops glitter in his ears. He's bare chested, bare assed, and barefoot, in a jockstrap and black leather chaps. A studded black leather dog collar is buckled about his neck, visual evidence of his slavery, and a short leash leads from that collar to Rick's left hand. His mouth alternates eagerly between Rick's boots. Inside his jock, his dick's stiff with the headiness of servitude.

Every time the Hokies score another touchdown, Rick allows Walker to stop licking leather long enough to eat a few chips. Four or five hit the floor, Walker eats them directly off the hardwood, then gratefully returns to Rick's boots, slurping over the heel, up along the toe, getting the leather shiny with spit. When Walker begs, Rick props his right ankle on his left knee so that Walker can more easily run his tongue over the gritty sole.

In the garage, Rick's pickup truck waits for the long drive up into the wilds of Highland County. It's packed with the playgear they'll need, along with the usual beer cooler and rifles, plus a few custom-made knives Walker crafts in his spare time and sells online. Many times they've hunted Highland together, but this weekend the prey will be not frightened deer but willing human. Walker's wife is out of town for three weeks, visiting her sister in Georgia, so he can afford a few bruises. He's young, he heals up fast; his nipples, back, and ass will be unmarked again by the time she returns.

Another Hokie touchdown, another Rick-whoop, another shower of chips that Walker lip-scoops up. When halftime comes around, Rick tugs on the leash; Walker obediently scoots closer on his knees. He wants to wrap his arms around Rick's waist but he knows better than to unclasp his hands without permission.

"You wanna get some barbeque on the way up the mountain? Easier than cooking once we get up there," Rick says, running a palm over his slave's smooth scalp, then tugging on the soul patch darkening Walker's chin.

Walker nods. Looking up at Rick's handsome face, his eyes brim with a barely suppressed wildness. It's the hunger of a starving junkyard dog suddenly, miraculously presented with a

T-bone steak. He's been aching for this weekend for months. He so rarely gets over to Rick's—for a quick bob on Rick's cock after work before Walker has to head home to Gena. Almost never does he get the full treatment he craves—several days' worth of abduction, torture, beating, rape—because of the marks Rick's teeth, hands, and belt are sure to leave, telltale marks that might ruin Walker's marriage.

Highland hunting trips in the fall—that tides them over, the nights they spend at Rick's cabin, the sex toned down to vanilla so as to leave Walker's body unmarred. They hunt deer and game birds those cold, pewter dawns. When Walker brings home meat, Gena's always pleased, without suspicion, having never seen *Brokeback Mountain*. Rick and Walker are both so masculine, such average rednecks, with a love of down-home food, country music, cheap beer, football, and weekend hunting trips, that she would never begin to imagine those Highland County nights when Rick shoves a balled-up boot sock in her husband's mouth and pushes his well-greased and very thick cock up her husband's ass. Queers, she knows, mince and wear pastels; a preacher's daughter schooled in sharp judgments and discerning eyes, she can spot a deviant a mile away.

"Okay, buddy, you ready for a drive?" Rick asks. The game's over, the Hokies have won, the chips are devoured, both men are hard with what's to come.

Walker nods. "First, man, I'd really like to suck your cock," he says with a note of pleading, staring at Rick's denimed crotch.

"Later," says Rick, unbuckling the leash. After several years of brief encounters, he's learned how to keep Walker hungry and in his place. "Once we get up the mountain, I'll pump your face till you slobber. Right now you should stretch." They both know Walker had better take advantage of his relative freedom while he can.

Walker obeys, dropping into several sets of push-ups, arcing through sit-ups. Rick savors the show, admiring the smooth chest and big nipples, the belly flexing with strain. If he had his way, Walker would be a divorcé and his full-time slave. Ever since Rick's father died, he's been sharply, painfully lonely, with only distant family left. Walker's visits thrill his body and fill his mind, giving him rich reasons to live. This is something he has yet to admit fully to himself, much less to the man working up a sweat at his feet.

"Stand," Rick says.

Walker does, bowing his head and closing his eyes.

"Hands behind your back."

There's the rip of duct tape being unpeeled—Rick doesn't like to fool with rope's complex knots, preferring tape's inescapable silvery simplicity. In just a few minutes, Walker's hands are bound, and strips of tape circle his moist and gleaming torso, securing his bulky arms to his sides. Rick hums, smoothing the silver against Walker's skin, cutting the tape with one of Walker's homemade hunting knives, then stands back to admire his handiwork. He can't get enough of Walker like this, half-naked and bound, standing there quietly, obediently, in his leather chaps. The rarity, brevity, and intensity of their encounters are driving him quietly crazy.

Rick shoulders on a biker jacket atop his vest—he knows how much Walker loves him in leather, the more the better—strokes the sleeve's scent of cowhide against Walker's face, then pulls a special surprise from a side pocket. "I wore these at work all week," Rick says, grinning. "They stink the way you like 'em." Rick knots the two dirty boot socks at the toes and rubs the cloth over Walker's mouth, pushing the knot against his nose.

Walker breathes deep, sucking in the smell. "Thanks, man," Walker whispers, and then the knot's between his teeth, the gag's pulled tight, its free ends tied behind his head. The rich taste of Rick's feet swamps his tongue. Walker bites down on rank cloth, sighing with satisfaction. He's damned lucky, he knows, to have found a Top this willing to meet his kinky requests, a Top who looks so damned fine in black leather and denim.

"You set?" Rick quizzes.

Walker nods.

"Tape and gag not too tight?"

Walker grunts a negative, shaking his head.

"Think you can take this all the way up the road?"

Walker nods.

For a good half a minute, the two men's stares interlock. Rick strokes Walker's cheek with a little more tenderness than he means to show, then, to make up for that weakness, roughly shoves Walker through the kitchen and into the garage. He pushes him into the Toyota Tacoma's broad bed, beneath the truck cap that will provide the concealment necessary for such a public scene, and onto a blow-up mattress they use for camping trips; it'll allow the captive some modicum of comfort on the winding drive up the mountain. Once his prisoner's stretched out, Rick tapes his bare ankles together, completing Walker's long-longed-for helplessness.

"You want a plug?" Rick asks, bending over his happy abductee, palm-kneading his smooth ass.

Walker grins around the sock gag, nods vigorously, rolls onto his belly, and lifts his ass. He loves having his hole filled, especially with Rick's cock, but a butt plug'll do until later tonight, when Walker finds himself getting pounded unmercifully on the cabin's bed. Rick fumbles through a toy bag, and pretty soon Walker's grunting with delight as the lubed plug slowly slides home. During their friendship, his hole has gone from "virgin" to "rapidly accommodating."

"Now these," growls Rick, pulling Japanese clover clamps from his jacket pocket.

Walker's brow creases. He groans and shakes his head, looking up at Rick with reluctance.

"Naw? Can't take these that long? Ah, come on, Walker? For me?" Rick's smile is beamingly wicked. He bends down, takes Walker's right nipple in his mouth, roughing it up a little till the tit's stiff and protuberant. Gena's been too busy going to church and burning hair to notice how prominent her husband's nipples have gotten over the last three years, since Rick and Walker met online at worldleathermen.com.

Rick has moved to the left nipple and mouth-maddened it, Walker nodding acquiescence. Triumphant, Rick eases the clamps on, then tugs on the connecting chain. Walker gasps into the smelly socks, his face distorting with pain. He knows his flesh will be on fire by the time they reach the cabin. He knows that's what Rick wants, so that's what Walker wants, too. This is only the first of several tortures upon which their desires will converge this blessed weekend.

Since Walker's still bare chested and barefoot, and since, warm as this autumn afternoon is, a chill will soon edge the air as the day declines, Rick, with some difficulty, awkward in the low-ceilinged space, works taped-tight Walker into a sleeping bag and zips him up. The solicitous Topman then wraps rope around Walker's cocoon at the torso and ankles, attaching him to the truck bed tie-downs with just enough leeway for Walker to shift his position slightly. Another layer of restraint, yes, plus it's a super-tortuous road up into the Alleghenies, and Rick doesn't want his captive to roll around too much, bouncing off metal walls. Any bruises Walker will receive today Rick will be providing.

Now the cooler's filled with ice and beer. Now Rick slams the tailgate shut, climbs into the cab, pushes in a Brad Paisley CD, and heads for the interstate. They're on their way.

II

Highland County has the highest elevation and the lowest population of any county in Virginia. It's one of the last fragments of Arcadia, albeit one threatened by Washington, D.C. developers and rising property taxes. Our boys' families settled here in the 1700s, managing a precarious living for several generations before moving down the mountain into Augusta County, to the growing city of Staunton with its easier life and numerous job opportunities. But the mountains are still in Rick's and Walker's blood. Staunton is work, propriety, routine. Highland is freedom: from Walker's wife, from their daily grinds, from the judging eyes of neighbors. Four-wheeling around the mountain roads or isolated in Rick's cabin in its quiet cove, they can be the complex and contradictory kind of men they really are: cocksucking, ass-fucking rednecks, kinky leather aficionados. They're too country for the city's urban gay ghettos, too queer for the fundamentalist-poisoned countryside. So they deceive, appearing to be something they're not for the sake of survival. But, ever so rarely, when they're together in the mountains, they can be honest, they can be home.

These things our boys sense without saying. Certainly Walker feels an excited rush of belonging, a sense of being driven deep into the magical, as he snuggles warmly, helpless as an infant in his roped-up swaddling, his sleeping-bag cocoon. He flexes his muscles against the tightness of the tape about his chest, arms, and wrists, and the constriction he feels is rapturous. His ass muscles work the thick plug, and it's pure bliss to have something filling him there. Occasionally he rolls onto his belly in order to rub his clamped nipples against the mattress, nudging his flesh from throbbing numbness back into agonizing fire. Inside his jock, his cock's curved and hard, in response both to his present bondage and to the thought of the brutal beating and rape to come. He could rub off on the mattress in about half a minute, as aroused as he is, but he knows better. He wants this bonfire in his body to last as long as possible.

Walker can't see where they're going as he sways on the mattress, feeling the curves of the road in the roped rocking of his makeshift hammock, but he knows this land so well he can pretty much guess where they are. First the smooth rush of the interstate. Then the relative flatness through Churchville. Then the long climb of the first great ridge, the truck moving through kiss-your-own-ass, polish-your-own-taillights curves, Walker tossing gently back and forth, very glad Rick's secured him so safely. Then the long descent into McDowell, where our boys have spent fine times at Battlefield Heritage Days festivals, striding around in dusters and cowboy hats, chatting with friends, tailgating with sandwiches and cheap beer. It's an odd feeling to be so much of this place and so much not. Ignorant of the boys' true natures, said friends would do anything for them. If somehow made aware of Rick and Walker's shared leather-passions, those same friends might shun them, pronouncing them sick and damned.

This unpleasant possibility becomes all too relevant when Walker feels the truck slow down, bump over ruts, and come to a stop. The rear window of the truck cab slides back, and there's Rick's voice over his head: "I'm fetching us barbeque. Keep real quiet."

Parking lot of the McDowell country store it's got to be, where the boys have grabbed many a tasty lunch. Slam of the truck door, crunch of Rick's boots across gravel.

Walker's sweating now. He's bound and gagged inches from

public gaze, only the thin truck cap between him and total humiliation. What if someone peering through the darkly tinted glass manages to see him? Would Rick be arrested for kidnapping? Then Walker would have to tell the truth. He imagines the headlines, and his balls contract with dread. "Perverts Caught in Midst of S&M Abduction." Walker lies there, mouth full of the taste of Rick's feet, thinking about what Gena would think if she saw him like this, what his loudly homophobic cousin might say, or his devout neighbors, or, worst of all, what his elderly parents might think. He's flushing with shame, wondering for the thousandth time why his own helplessness gets him so hard, wondering why a man as strong and butch as he—a man obsessed with strength, control, and independence, a weightlifter, a biker, a blacksmith—why such a man aches to submit. He's seeing no answer, just mystery as dark and glossy as the black leather he loves.

Voices now, just outside the tailgate. Walker keeps perfectly still, listening. Sweat's beading his upper lip, nesting in his armpits and palms, welling up on his thighs, beneath his tight leather chaps. Rick's talking to someone in the parking lot. A woman's voice, one Walker half recognizes. Something about the next auction scheduled up here, a house near Monterey.

Then the stranger's voice mentions Walker's name, and the voice isn't strange any more. It's Gertie, who runs the historical society in McDowell. She's asking about Walker's knife-making, wondering if he's still forging those antler-handled daggers everyone admires. Heart pounding, Walker bites down on his gag, pants a little, closes his eyes, and prays.

Rick laughs. Then there's gravel-crunch, intonations of farewell. The driver's door opens, the truck shifts a bit with Rick's weight.

"Did you piss yourself?" Rick chuckles through the cab window.

Walker breathes out a deep sigh and grunts "Fuck you" into his mouthful of cloth.

The engine starts, and they're on the move again. Walker rolls over, pushing his chest against the mattress till the pain in his clamped nipples eases fear from his brain. There's another great ridge to come, then descent into Monterey, then on to Hightown, then a few miles out Botkin Run, and they'll be home.

III

Rick's gentle with him, dragging him carefully out of the truck. He leaves Walker in his by-now-very-moist cocoon, there on the lawn, while he sheds his jacket to unload the truck. Walker looks up at the sky, periwinkle at the summit, indigo at the edges, bisected by a sugar maple limb aflame with autumn's burnt orange. He looks up at the dark crags of Devil's Backbone, the huge rock formation that sharpens the horizon above the cove. He rolls on his side, off his aching wrists, and stares into the grass, palisades of green teeming with little lives he normally gives no thought to. Today he feels as small as they are, a slave with his cheek pressed against the earth, pain smoldering in long-bound hands and feet, in metal-chewed nipples and strained shoulders. Today, through Rick, God will lift him up from exposure, damnation, and the dark boil of self, into cleansing punishment, into the high air of the mountains, into the flay of sunlight and salvation.

When Walker's eyes grow wet, he closes them. Now there's only sound: Rick's whistle, the thump of cooler on porch, and, farther away, wind in leaves, purling of the creek, a hawk's remote *cheeee*.

The fat knot of the sock-gag's pulled from Walker's mouth, down over his chin. His eyes open. Rick's boot-toe nudges his cheek.

"You wanna be beat, or you wanna eat?" Rick laughs at his own rhyme. Childish wordplay has always delighted him. He's giddy seeing Walker so defenseless. He wants this weekend's possession never to end.

"I ain't real hungry...." Walker's voice catches, his cheeks flush crimson.

Sound of the sleeping bag's zipper descending. Cool air washes over Walker's sweaty chest. Rick rolls him onto his back and stands astride his hips. Yes, here's the religion Walker needs: this god with flaming red fur, black leather vest, and biker cap looming above him, pushing the stern sole of a boot against Walker's face, demanding reverence. Walker groans, lapping the tread, tasting grass, tasting dirt.

Rick stares down at him, almost sadly. "So you wanna be hurt bad, boy?"

"God. God. Yes, Sir. God," Walker murmurs. He hasn't had a full weekend with Rick for nine months. He needs to howl.

Rick pulls out the bowie knife, bone-handled, one of Walker's best pieces, forged for Rick's last birthday. The tape around Walker's ankles is cut. He's rolled onto his belly. He groans loudly as the plug's eased from his ass. Suddenly the leash is there again, snapped onto Walker's dog collar. He's neck-tugged to his feet, and now he's being dragged gasping and stumbling into thick woods back of the house.

IV

The bark's rough against Walker's naked chest, cheek, and brow. It makes his still-clamped tits ache anew. There's duct tape over his eyes, but he can feel late afternoon sunlight slanting over his shoulders, back, and ass, here in the clearing between pines. There's duct tape over his mouth, but he can taste Rick's fresh piss in the rag stuffing his cheeks. His arms are wrapped tightly around the hickory; his hands are crossed at the wrists and taped together on the trunk's far side. His chaps have been pulled down to his ankles, exposing his white ass. His skin's a parchment upon which Rick's about to compose.

There's nothing quite like the sound a leather belt makes when jerked from its loops. Walker hears it and shudders. He clenches his fingers into fists and hugs the tree harder.

Rick stands behind Walker, belt hanging from his right hand. He relishes those times when Walker's blindfolded, when he can study his part-time slave's beautiful body and know Walker can't see the deep need, the unspoken love in Rick's eyes. For a year now he's been biting back a beggar's words, every time Walker's head or hole gulps Rick's dick. Nothing's sweeter than what they've found together. Why won't Walker leave his fucking wife?

Rick shakes his head, clearing it for the purpose at hand, and swings. The leather strap arcs through the air with perfect, practiced accuracy. Walker groans.

Rick swings again, harder. Walker shouts.

Rick swings again, harder. Walker screams. What wildlife's nestled nearby—crows, chipmunks, deer—moves off, giving our lovers their privacy.

V

"More?" says Rick, his lips brushing Walker's scalp.

Walker flinches under Rick's touch. Tenderness is a shock after such lengthy brutality. He's panting, his heart's racing. A thin trembling spreads over his skin. Tears moisten the tape over his eyes, his rag-distended cheeks. He's never been more alive, more thankful, more awake.

Rick's hands gently range over the welts he's made, a good half an hour's work, across his captive's shoulders, back, and buttocks. He feels pride, guilt, fear, awe, and delight. Walker's naked suffering is the greatest beauty Rick's ever known.

"We've been this far before, boy. You wanna go farther?" Rick whispers, kissing belt-reddened shoulders.

Walker shudders, straining his wrists against the tight tape.

"You swore you were ready for more, boy. You swore you wanted to sob this time. You swore you wanted to bleed," Rick whispers, hairy chest pressed against sweat-streaked back.

Walker sighs, pressing his taped face against the tree.

"You begged for that, remember? Said you were ready. Ready to be broken. We've never gone that far before. You still want that? You want that now? You ready for more? Can my boy take more? I'll bet my boy can take more," Rick whispers, wiping the wet of tears off Walker's cheeks.

Rick's never broken Walker. Both men wonder what will happen if Walker's broken. Both men wonder if, broken, Walker will stay.

Walker nods, arching his ass against Rick's crotch, spreading his legs. About his bare feet breeze tousles the gold of fallen leaves.

"More, please, Sir," he mutters into the piss-bitter rag. He wants to be unknit, undone, hung and nailed to the cross of his own flesh. He wants to be a heap of broken wood smoking and flickering at Rick's feet, charred logs and oak ash that Rick's boots grind down and mingle into black mountain earth.

"You got it. Let loose, buddy. Scream as much as you want. Between that rag-and-tape gag and the goodly number of miles between us and the nearest neighbors, no one's gonna hear you."

Stepping back, Rick retrieves the belt from the grass and doubles it over. He licks the leather, smiling, watching the way Walker's shoulders heave and his thighs shake. Rick's forearm is throbbing with exertion; he has about fifteen minutes left in him. That should more than do it.

VI

The salve is cool, scented with aloe. Rick's spreading it over purpling bruises and swollen welt-ridges on Walker's shoulders, back, and buttocks.

Sprawled on his belly, hands cuffed before him, arms hugging a pillow, wearing nothing but his dog collar and jockstrap, Walker grunts with pleasure beneath the soothing touch. Wounds absorb the medicine, fire ebbs. The Lord beateth down and the Lord healeth, that's what he wants to say. Instead he keeps silent except for an occasional "Oh, man, thanks. Oh, man, that's great." He's being tended to on the little bed that was Rick's in his boyhood. Rick would like to get a bigger mattress for them to share for those rare times Walker's up here—this bed's a little too snug for two grown guys—but he can't afford it just yet. With rising taxes, he can barely afford to hold on to this property. If he loses this land, in his family for two hundred years, he won't know how to live with himself.

The barbeque's been devoured, the beer stash has been considerably depleted. Our boys have spent a relaxed evening watching war movies and munching popcorn. The lengthy break between DVDs Walker's spent on his knees, enjoying a rough face-fucking. Solicitous, Rick's salved his slave's skin several times since the beating, and now, just before bed, is doing it again.

Finished comforting the wounds he created, Rick rises, wipes off his hands on a camo bandana, then strips off his boots and jeans. Wearing only the leather vest he knows Walker loves so well, he climbs into bed, squeezing in beside Walker in the tight, warm space. Walker rolls onto his side, his back to his master;

Rick wraps an arm around his slave's waist, pulls him close, and tugs the sheet up over them.

They lie there quietly. A pine-scented candle gleams on the bedside table. The window's open a crack, so as to give them the night chill's excuse to snuggle and the barely audible sound of the creek. They're thinking about the scene today, their most extreme ever: Walker's wild thrashing, his gagged and broken begging, the blood streaking his back, his body heaving with sobs, his tear-wet cheeks staining the hickory bark dark. They're remembering the way Rick finally dropped the belt, his arm exhausted with ecstasy's efforts; the way, in spite of the cautious distances demanded by this virus-plagued age, he licked Walker's blood off his back; the way he wiped snot from his nose, stroking him while he shook and cried; the way Rick cut him loose, carefully pulled the tape from his wrists, eyes, and mouth, tugged out the piss-cloth, and fell into the fallen leaves with him, there in the shadow of Devil's Backbone, holding him till his weeping ceased.

Both know what's next. Both need to be filled further.

Rick knots the camo bandana between Walker's teeth and loosely chains his cuffed hands to the headboard. Walker's rolled onto his belly, on a pile of pillows, and Rick's cock, well lubed, is thrust up Walker's ass. It's a ride slow and gentle at first, then rough and rapid. No condom, since they're both negative, and since neither has messed with other men since they've met.

Rick pounds Walker till his hole is burning. He clamps his hand firmly over Walker's mumbled pleas and keeps pounding him even when Walker begs him to stop. As much as Walker protests, they both want him so sore tomorrow that he has to sit on a pillow in the truck cab on the way back to Staunton. Neither would have it any other way. Rick takes his time, wanting it to last, slowing down and speeding up, loving the way

Walker futilely fights him. Walker bucks and twists, tugging on his bonds till the headboard creaks, whimpering with discomfort and delight. Finally, with a gritted-teeth growl, Rick shoots up his slave's ass.

Walker won't be allowed to come tonight, or during the similar savage fucking he'll take tomorrow morning, when Rick wakes ready for more. Tomorrow afternoon, just before they leave their sanctuary, Walker will be taped to a chair, gagged with a soft black leather strap, and edged for an hour or so before he's finally permitted to shoot the huge load that extended bondage inspires in him. After his slave's unbound, Rick will command him to lick his own semen off the hardwood floor. On his hands and knees, Walker will happily comply, lapping till his lips glisten.

Tonight, though, they curl together exhausted, so happy to be skin to skin. Rick leaves the bandana tied in Walker's mouth and leaves his hands cuffed and chained to the bed. If Walker needs to piss in the middle of the night, Rick will simply lock his mouth around Walker's cock and greedily gulp. He'll take every taste of Walker he can get for as long as he can.

It's almost midnight. While starlight and the shadows of tree limbs shift across the cabin roof and over the lawn, both men slowly slip toward sleep. Walker sleepily chews the wet cloth tied between his teeth the way an infant would a breast; Rick sleepily thumbs Walker's raw right nipple the way he would a banjo string. Walker mutters, "I need owning bad." Rick, making out the words despite the muffle of cloth, kisses a welt on Walker's back.

Both men know that several ridge tops over sleep country people of another sort, people who claim to be Love's dedicatees—followers of a previous beautiful, bound, sacrificed man—but who, given the knowledge and the power, would burn down this house with Rick and Walker inside and find their deaths cause for celebration. Both men know that down Botkin Run, in Monterey, sleep wealthy men who want to make Highland County a land of scenic subdivisions for upscale city folks tired of D.C.'s frenetic madness, full of big fancy homes no locals could ever afford.

Neither man knows how long what they have will last. Neither knows what Walker might say tomorrow morning, if Rick gets up the guts to admit how he feels and begs Walker to stay. Neither knows if Walker will ever overcome his shame, his fear of how his parents, in-laws, friends, and coworkers might react if they knew him truly, if he turned his back on Shenandoah propriety and left Gena for a man. Neither knows what might happen if Walker began to share Rick's little Staunton house, if they could spend every weekend together in Highland. Neither knows, but both sense, in some clairvoyant corner of their minds, that a passion of this depth will come for neither of them again.

Without answers, they snuggle closer as October's constellations sweep across the sky. Rick, mumbling drowsily, asks if Walker will help him chop some wood tomorrow between leather scenes. Walker smiles, nods, and commences to snore. Rick joins in ten seconds later.

Outside, earlier than predicted, the season's first frost forms. It spreads over the hood of Rick's truck, on the split-rail fence abutting the road, over the zinnias Rick planted last spring, on the grass where Walker lay cocooned, and, high above the cove, on the sharp stone ridge of Devil's Backbone. By dawn, a fine dusting of crystal has edged everything, dead-gray as woodstove ash. Surrounding the warmth of cabin and conjoined bodies, the cold world glitters: fangs, powdered mica, starlight solidified.

Neither man knows nor cares. Just after daybreak, Walker's

ass rubs Rick's cock. Rick wakes, slicks himself with spit. They make love again, they cuddle close and fall back to sleep, unwilling to leave a nest so cozy. Outside, fingers of sunlight stroke the earth. The merciful melt slowly spreads, the shadow of Devil's Backbone retreats.

In late morning, our boys rise. The master frees his slave; the slave brews coffee, fries bacon, bakes biscuits, scrambles eggs. Both men watch the kitchen clock, counting the hours left to them before they must return to the workaday world. In the forest, beneath the hickory where Walker was bound and beaten, on the blood-stippled gold of fallen leaves the frost dissolves.

ABOUT THE AUTHORS

When **SHANE ALLISON** is not giving blow jobs through the bathroom glory holes of universities to college boys, he is writing stories about the college boys he has given blow jobs to through the bathroom glory holes of universities in Florida and beyond. His stories have gone on to grace the pages of *Best Black Gay Erotica, Dorm Porn 2, Ultimate Gay Erotica 2006* and *2007, Truckers, Cowboys, Hustlers, Sexiest Soles* and *Best Gay Erotica 2007*. He is the editor of *Hot Cops: Gay Erotic Stories*. Thugs, punks, nerds, married men and scarred up, skinny white boys can drop him emails and nudie pics at starsissy42@hotmail.com.

BILL BRENT's sex-and-drugs memoir, "This Insane Allure," comprises one-seventh of *Entangled Lives: Memoirs of 7 Top Erotic Authors*. His nonfiction article, "Martin Luther Goes Bowling," appears in *Everything You Know about God Is Wrong*. His short story, "Other People's Women," is part of *Five-Minute*

Erotica, Vol. 2. "Yummy," included here, is from his third novel, in progress. Bill recently completed his first novel, about a young whoreboy who runs away (from his clients and girlfriend) to join the circus. Follow Bill's antics at LitBoy.com.

DAN CULLINANE spent ten years as a shill for a major gay media company in Los Angeles, before heading off for bigger adventures behind the wheel of his pickup. After many many miles and many many words for such publications as *Frontiers* and *Publishers Weekly*, he has taken up residence on a farm in Eastern Tennessee for a spell of teaching.

DOUG HARRISON's erotic ruminations appear in zines, a dozen anthologies, and his memoir, *In Search of Ecstasy* (www.shadowsacrament.com/contents_2.1.htm), most of which complement his opera fairydom and offset his PhD in optical engineering. Doug was active in San Francisco's leather scene and the Modern Primitives movement. He appears in videos, photo shoots, and an AIDS Emergency Fund's Bare Chest Calendar. He is a member of the Chicago Hellfire Club. He lives in warm Hawaii, where his most difficult sartorial decision is which color jock or thong to wear.

SHAUN LEVIN's collection of stories, *A Year of Two Summers*, was published in 2005. A novella, *Seven Sweet Things*, was published in 2003. His stories appear in anthologies as diverse as *Between Men, Modern South African Stories, Boyfriends from Hell, Best Gay Erotica*, and *The Slow Mirror: New Fiction by Jewish Writers*. He is the editor of *Chroma: A Queer Literary Journal*. See more at shaunlevin.com and chromajournal.co.uk.

JEFF MANN's books include two collections of poetry, *Bones Washed with Wine* and *On the Tongue*; a book of personal essays, *Edge;* a novella, *Devoured*, included in *Masters of Midnight: Erotic Tales of the Vampire;* a collection of poetry and memoir, *Loving Mountains, Loving Men*; and a volume of short fiction, *A History of Barbed Wire*, winner of a Lambda Literary Award. He teaches creative writing at Virginia Tech in Blacksburg, Virginia.

COLIN PENPANK, a gay writer of the 1970s, is a character in an unfinished novel by Nicol Knappen. Knappen has spent most of his career in one or another aspect of publishing, usually as some kind of editor. He's also written many informative articles and essays about things that, he says, are of interest to hardly anyone. He feels that another writer's self-assessment also works for him: "personality—nil." "Sharkskin" is the first fiction he's published.

CHRISTOPHER PIERCE is the author of the novel *Rogue: Slave*, published by StarBooks Press. His erotic fiction has been published in more than twenty anthologies, including *Ultimate Gay Erotica 2005, 2006, 2007* and *2008*. He coedited the *Fetish Chest Trilogy* anthologies with Rachel Kramer Bussel. Visit Chris at www.christopherpierceerotica.com.

THOMAS ROCHE's short stories have appeared in hundreds of magazines, websites, and anthologies including the *Best American Erotica* series, the *Best New Erotica* series, and many others. He is the public relations manager of Kink.com and blogs about sex, drugs, and cryptozoology at www.thomasroche.com.

HOREHOUND STILLPOINT's work has been seen in coffee shops, bars, and onstage, and has been collected in many anthologies of poetry, porn, and memoir. He lives in San Francisco.

AARON TRAVIS is the pen name of novelist Steven Saylor. His first erotic story appeared in 1979 in *Drummer* magazine, which he later edited. Travis retired from writing erotica in the 1990s, but his work, such as the gladiator novel *Slaves of the Empire,* continues to be reprinted. His website is at stevensaylor.com/aarontravis.

KARL VON UHL is the author of various smutty works that have appeared in the *Best Gay Erotica* series, the anthologies *Rough Stuff, Roughed Up, Bearotica, Tough Guys,* and others. He lives in Southern California.

ALANA NOËL VOTH is a single mom who lives in Oregon with her ten-year-old son, two cats, and several freshwater fish. Her fiction has appeared in *Best Gay Erotica 2008, 2007* and *2004; Best American Erotica 2005; Where the Boys Are: Urban Gay Erotica; I Is for Indecent,* and online at Cleansheets, Blithe House Quarterly, The Big Stupid Review, Oysters and Chocolate, Eclectica Magazine, and Literary Mama.

XAN WEST is the pseudonym of a New York City BDSM educator and writer. Xan's work can be found in *Best SM Erotica 2, Got a Minute?, Love at First Sting* and the forthcoming *Men on the Edge*. Xan has a particular love for boots, punching, and shiny sharp things. Xan's story, "Willing," has been searching for a publisher since 2004, and is glad to have found such a good home. Xan can be reached at xan_west@yahoo.com.

ELAZARUS WILLS is a journalist, artist, gay erotica writer, and used bookstore owner living in rural western Colorado with his partner of twenty years. He works with leather from time to time but has never actually made a whole saddle. Recent stories have appeared in Clean Sheets, Ruthie's Club, and in several gay fiction anthologies including *Animal Attraction*.

THOM WOLF is the author of the erotic novels *Words Made Flesh* and *The Chain*. Over the past decade, his work has also appeared in a number of anthologies, including *Ultimate Gay Erotica 2007* and *Bi Guys*. He's hard at work studying literature and creative writing, and lives in England.

ABOUT THE EDITOR

SIMON SHEPPARD is the editor of *Homosex: Sixty Years of Gay Erotica,* and the author of *In Deep, Sex Parties 101, Kinkorama: Dispatches From the Front Lines of Perversion,* and *Hotter Than Hell and Other Stories,* which won an Erotic Authors Association Award as best short-story collection of the year. He is also, with M. Christian, coeditor of the anthologies *Rough Stuff* and *Roughed Up,* and his work has appeared in upward of three hundred books and magazines, including many editions of *The Best American Erotica* and many, many editions of *Best Gay Erotica.* He also writes the syndicated column "Sex Talk" and the online serial The Dirty Boys Club. He lives in San Francisco with his beloved partner, stacks of books, and a small collection of floggers, and can be found virtually at www.simonsheppard.com.